THE HIRED HAND

by

Melissa Schroeder

WHISKEY CREEK PRESS
www.whiskeycreekpress.com

Published by
WHISKEY CREEK PRESS

Whiskey Creek Press
PO Box 51052
Casper, WY 82605-1052
www.whiskeycreekpress.com

ISBN 1-978-59374-024-5

Credits
Cover Artist: Scott Carpenter
Editor: Chere Gruver

Printed in the United States of America

Dedication

To Terry Wilde Spear whose tireless help, encouragement and critiques enabled me to write *The Hired Hand* and so many more. You're the best critique partner a gal could ever have.

AND

To Les, who did the laundry, listened to me whine, and always believed. You are my lover, my friend, and my favorite research tool. I push and you stay the course. I love you.

Chapter 1

"You hired me a what?" Marlow Smith asked from behind clenched teeth.

"Marlow," Joey said, as if talking to a five-year-old. "It's a birthday present. You need to cut loose. You need a break."

Marlow stared at her best friend and administrative assistant, wondering if she'd taken to drinking in the middle of the afternoon. Joey stood before her, a red spandex excuse for a dress in her hands, a calm look on her perfect face. *Yep, she'd been hitting the bottle.*

"A break? A break does not include hiring a gigolo for the night!"

With an exasperated sigh, Joey tossed the dress on the bed. "Listen, hon, you've been working like crazy the last few months. The problems with the company...well, you need to get laid."

"Yeah, I know, but...a gigolo? Josephenia Vernon! A gigolo!"

"Listen, you haven't dated anyone since Vic. You need this, and Clarice owed me."

Only Joey would have a childhood friend who became the owner of an escort service. Marlow didn't even want to contemplate what favor Clarice owed her. "There is no way on earth this is going to happen, Joey."

"Marlow—"

"No, I'm not the type of woman who needs…"

Joey placed a hand on each hip and raised an eyebrow.

"Okay, I'm not the type who wants a gigolo." Joey snorted but kept her mouth shut. "Now, how much time do we have?"

Joey's eyes widened. "I thought you said you didn't want to go."

"I don't want a gigolo but we're going to the club and firing him. I can't let him sit there all night, wondering what happened."

"Marlow—"

"No. We're going and I'm going to stand there while you'll explain *you're* the one who hired him and I don't desire to avail myself of his services for the evening!" She still couldn't believe Joey pulled this! "When were we supposed to meet him?"

"Ten. And it was supposed to be *you*, not both of us."

Marlow glanced at her watch. She had less than an hour. There was no reason to panic. They'd meet the man and tell him what happened. "I'm going to take a quick shower. I feel funky." She grabbed her toiletry bag. "Don't try anything while I'm gone."

She emerged from the shower ten minutes later, the grime of the two-hour car trip after a long day at work washed away. Immediately, she realized her clothes were no longer sitting on the counter where she had placed them. She shrugged it off, thinking Joey must have grabbed them up. After hurriedly drying her hair, she wrapped the towel around her body and walked out the door into the empty bedroom.

"Joey?" Silence. "Joey?"

Uneasiness crept into her stomach, souring the contents. "Joey?" Still nothing.

She walked into the living room and the worry increased when she found it empty as well. Thinking to get dressed as fast as possible, she dashed into the bedroom. Only her suitcase was no longer sitting on the luggage rack.

"Joey," she groaned. She paced the room, chewing her thumbnail. Joey was outrageous, unpredictable, and outspoken but Marlow never thought she'd leave her in a Dallas hotel room without anything to wear. Thinking there might be something in the dresser, she ran to it and began opening drawers. But, as she found each one empty, her panic increased and the pounding in her head became unbearable.

Every bit of her clothing was gone, including her underwear. She couldn't believe Joey had done this. They'd been best friends almost since the moment she'd hired Joey. Marlow shook her head. Even with her over-the-top personality Joey would never leave her in Dallas without clothes. At least Marlow didn't think she would.

Marlow wandered back into the living area and realized the closet door was ajar. She walked to it, hoping Joey had just left her things in there. Her heart sank when she pulled it open and found only the red dress Joey had bought her hanging there. Draped over one shoulder, was a pair of off-black thigh highs and a lacey red pushup bra over the other. Resting on the floor was a pair of matching stiletto pumps.

A piece of hotel stationary had been stuffed into the top of the dress. She yanked it out of the dress, dread settling into her stomach.

Marlow,

You can kill me when you get back to Abilene. Mr. Jones will be at the club wearing a green shirt, sitting at the bar. He's supposed to be over six feet, blonde with green eyes. Don't do anything I wouldn't do.

-J

Marlow wadded up the piece of paper and threw it in the wastebasket. How could Joey do this to her? Marlow didn't need a break. What she needed was a new administrative assistant!

She looked at the dress and shook her head. It would barely cover her butt. There was no way she was going to meet a hired escort dressed in *that*. She didn't care if he sat there all night. She really didn't.

* * * *

"I'm very sorry, Mr. Jones, but I have no need for an escort tonight," Marlow said with a frown.

No, that didn't sound right. How did one fire a gigolo and not sound like an idiot?

She hurried down the street to the club and sighed when the neon sign came into view a block ahead. The flashing red and white letters pierced the dark street, illuminating the entrance. With each step she took, the stiletto heels jarred her feet. When she returned to her hotel room tonight, she'd consign the red torture devices to hell and soak her feet for a month.

She paid the doorman and hurried into the nightclub. Goosebumps exploded across her skin when she stepped from the sultry Texas heat and into the cool air of the night-club — a glaring reminder that her chest was almost as bare as her back. She shivered and crossed her arms.

She was going to kill Joey when she got a hold of her. The red spandex sheath clung to her hips and rear end, highlighting every extra jiggle. With each step, the hem of it rose and she hoped it wasn't rising above the top of the lacy thigh highs Joey had left for her.

Marlow mentally reminded herself of Joey's description of the man she hired: at least six feet tall, blonde hair, green eyes, and wearing a green shirt. She glanced around the room and was surprised when more than a couple pairs of eyes stared back, inspecting her like a piece of meat from the stockyards.

Usually, Marlow Jane Smith did not attract attention. Small-boned and short, she lacked the feminine attributes most men thought of as sexy. Well, at least what beer commercials told them was sexy. Marlow rubbed her arms, and scrutinized the men who were line dancing. Hmmm, lots of good-looking blondes, none of them were wearing a green shirt.

Unwilling to abandon her search, she decided to make one trip around the club. Marlow walked past a few of the tables, looking over the men but not making eye contact. The ache in her feet intensified with each step.

Joey had left those clothes, knowing Marlow would never let the man sit there all night. All the rules of etiquette were so ingrained in her she had to tell a male hooker she wouldn't need his services for the evening. If her compulsion to do exactly the right thing weren't so sad, she'd have laughed at the foolish thought.

She glanced around the club again, and almost shrunk under the scrutiny. *Ignore them,* she could almost hear Joey whisper in her ear. Determined to make it through the crowd and find Mr. Jones, she threw her shoulders back, causing her chest to rise, and raised her chin a notch. Then she saw him—sitting at the end of the bar with a redhead practically in his lap.

Marlow glanced at the woman, who gave her a dirty look, and then cut a look at the man.

Although he draped his arm across the back of the other woman's chair, he was staring at Marlow. She shivered as his gaze dropped down from her eyes, then to her shoulders and finally, her breasts. He continued his frank assessment down to her toes and then all the way back up. One corner of his mouth quirked, and an eyebrow was raised.

Before she could allow herself to contemplate how to approach her *paid* escort, he leaned over and whispered something into the woman's ear. Her smile faded and she shot Marlow another dirty look before flouncing away. Marlow glanced back to the man to find him gazing directly at her, his intense stare causing a heated blush to rise from her chest to her face.

Marlow walked slowly toward the end of the bar. She inhaled deeply and took a seat.

Be short and to the point.

"Mr. Jones, I think there's been some kind of mistake."

"Darlin'" he said, his voice as smooth as the whiskey he was drinking, "I'm not Mr. Jones. Although, I have to say," his eyes traveled down her body again and returned to her face, "I wouldn't mind taking his place." His sensuous lips curved and a couple dimples appeared.

She swallowed twice, gathering the courage to explain who she was. If she were in a boardroom in her own clothes, she wouldn't have had a problem confronting this man. Joey would flirt. Marlow rarely used flirtation. She never understood the finer points. Uncomfortable in any kind of man-woman situation, Marlow had failed miserably during her last stint on the dating scene. Never one to spend a Saturday night dateless, Joey badgered Marlow about finding a man, but Marlow avoided the discussion. She wanted to find a nice man who wanted to settle down. Marlow wasn't looking for a great passion. A dependable man, who wanted a quiet life with a wife and kids, was fine with her.

Joey thought she was crazy hence the escort.

He sat there, smiling at her, with those blasted dimples and an expectant look on his face.

"I know that's not your real name," she said, aware her Texas accent had grown more pronounced, "but there's been a mistake." He leaned forward, placing his arms on the bar, confusion darkening his green eyes. "I'm not the one who hired you, but I promise you'll get paid."

"Hired me?" he almost croaked.

"Yes," she said nodding, never allowing her eyes to wander to his open collar. A glimpse of golden brown hair curled in the V of his green shirt, and she fought the urge to tell him to button it up. At the same time, she had to resist reaching out to comb her fingers through those curls and feel the hard, hot muscle of his chest beneath them. *Why the hell was she thinking about his muscles?* "A friend thought that it would be a good idea to hire a man for me on my thirtieth birthday." She watched the dimples disappear. "Like I said, you'll get paid, I just don't see a reason for buying a man." *Even if he's built like a Greek god.*

He raised one thick, dark blonde eyebrow. "Well, at least let me buy you a drink."

She searched his expressionless face. Other than that perusal, he didn't show any more interest in her than he probably would have shown any other woman. He definitely wasn't overcome with lust so she said, "Sure, but then I really have to go."

* * * *

Liam Campbell stared at the petite woman beside him while she placed her order with the bartender. He felt free to look his fill while she leaned over the bar and ordered a club soda.

She *was* little. Small-boned and delicate, she couldn't be more than five-foot-two in her stocking feet. When he first saw her walk through the club, he'd thought she was taller. But the killer f-me heels she wore gave the illusion of height.

It didn't really matter. He loved all women. Tall, short, skinny, fat, any hair color, he loved them. He didn't personally love as many as his brother, Heath, claimed he did, but he was never at a loss for a date. He had strict guidelines about who ended up in his bed. Women he dated knew the score: a fun time, no strings attached.

He'd been sitting at the end of the bar waiting for Heath, thinking that he'd stood Liam up for work once again. He was about to call it a night, after he called Heath to gripe at him, when a flash of red caught his eye.

What struck him first about her was her demeanor as she carefully stepped through the crowd, avoiding contact with most of the people there. She walked across the floor like a deb on the night of her coming out, but dressed like sin.

The red dress she wore left little to the imagination. It clung to every curve she had. Her mass of inky hair cascaded down her back, making him want to bury his face in it. He couldn't make out the color of her eyes, but they looked to be some shade between blue and gray, surrounded by thick lashes. She wore little makeup, but her bee-stung lips were painted almost the same shade of red as her dress and she had the cutest little overbite. At the moment, she was worrying her bottom lip when he realized he was staring at her mouth, wondering what it tasted like.

He met her gaze and saw apprehension. She may have strutted through the bar like a self-assured woman, but she was nervous. *Well, who wouldn't be when trying to tell a paid escort to take a hike?*

"Now, Ms.——" he said, leaving it hanging and waited for an answer.

"Smith. Jane Smith."

He chuckled. "Smith and Jones?"

She sat up straighter, thrusting her chest out. "My real name is Smith." Ah, interesting. Maybe Ms. Smith was using another first name.

"Ms. Smith, why don't you explain why you don't need an escort for the evening?" He knew he was attractive to the opposite sex and enjoyed when a woman was bold enough to approach him, just as much as he enjoyed chasing after them. But in all his years, he'd never had one of them try to pick him up, claiming she'd paid him for the evening. No, *someone else* had paid.

She heaved a sigh, drawing his eyes to her breasts again. Not huge and spectacular, although the pushup bra he knew she wore did wonders for them. No, they weren't big, but he'd bet the farm they were beautiful. They were probably petite, just like the rest of her, but smooth as a baby's bottom with pink nipples that would taste so sweet. He looked back up to her face, and even through the smoke of the club, he could see her blush.

"I don't need an escort. A very misguided and soon to be unemployed friend decided I needed a man for the evening. I wouldn't have come, but I couldn't leave you sitting here waiting for me."

"No?"

"No. It's just not done." Her voice had taken on an icy edge but that probably had to do with his eyes dipping down to look at her cleavage every few seconds. He really wanted to see those breasts. He wanted to see if they were as smooth and ivory as the rest of her skin. At that moment, Liam knew he was going to seduce the birthday girl.

"Ms. Smith, maybe we could go somewhere a little quieter?"

"No."

"Excuse me?"

"No, Mr. Jones, I don't think that's a good idea."

He leaned back in his chair, trying to look nonchalant. Not a man used to rejection from any woman, Liam stared at the woman for a minute or two. She squirmed under his scrutiny, and he felt a little satisfaction.

"I appreciate the offer, really, but I need to get back. I have to get up and drive home tomorrow and truthfully," she said leaning forward just a bit, allowing him a wonderful view down her dress, "I'm usually in bed by ten o'clock."

He looked into her eyes to see if she was flirting with him, but saw only honesty.

"I'm usually in bed by ten, too." He found her attempt to give him the brush off irritating. So what if he wasn't her paid escort for the evening?

She jerked away from him and she blushed again.

"I'm sure you *are* in bed, Mr. Jones, but *I* am usually asleep."

He looked at her, nonplussed for a second, and then laughed. So the sweet little woman had some bite to her. *Sweet and spicy. Even better.* He was mentally rubbing his hands together.

"Besides, your *friend* wouldn't be happy if you left just yet."

Liam wondered how she knew he was meeting his brother, but he noticed her looking over his shoulder. He turned around and saw the redhead who had told him she could tie a cherry stem with her tongue. He smiled at her and her friends but turned back around.

"Oh, I just met her. She sat down next to me and bought me a drink."

"I don't doubt it, Mr. Jones." She stood and gathered her purse. "I really understand that you're worried about your payment, but there's no reason. Joey will make sure you're paid in full for the night. She's very good friends with Clarice."

He shrugged. Since he had no idea who Joey, or Clarice, was, he figured it really didn't matter.

"Thank you so much for understanding, Mr. Jones, but I really need to go."

"I'll tell you what," he said, standing, "why don't we have a cup of coffee? My treat. That way I won't feel guilty about getting paid for tonight. There's a great little diner within walking distance."

Okay, so that was lame. He really didn't want this woman to leave. At least, not without him. He pulled his wallet out and threw a couple of tens on the bar.

She looked up at him. He thought he saw a flash of annoyance in those big blue eyes, but it disappeared behind a mask of polite manners.

"You would feel guilty about taking money you didn't earn?" she asked.

"Yes. My parents drummed things like that into my head." He used her sense of right and wrong to get her to come with him. He knew it was really beneath him, but, hell, whoever heard of someone so bent on doing the right thing they show up at a nightclub, dressed like a wet dream come true, to make sure the hired escort for the evening didn't waste his time waiting on her?

She stared at him, as if trying to guess if he was handing her a load of manure, and then she smiled her first real smile. Her face really lit up when she smiled, and a slice of warmth slid into his gut. He knew there was no way in hell he was going to let her go back to the hotel room to celebrate alone. She was going to celebrate with him.

"Okay," she said, still smiling, "but only one cup of coffee."

* * * *

Marlow took a sip of coffee and almost sighed out loud. The hot liquid slid down her throat and warmed her belly. She brought the cup back up to her mouth, closed her eyes, and inhaled the deep aroma.

"You seem to be taking an inordinate amount of pleasure in drinking that cup of coffee."

She opened her eyes and studied her coffee companion, her hired gigolo. *Talk about warming my belly.* His golden brown hair, mussed by the Texas wind, curled around the top of his collar, the tips of it kissed by the sun. His green eyes, a shade lighter than she thought they were, looked exotic against his tanned skin. The skin around them crinkled around the corners each time he smiled. She figured, given his demeanor and his profession, the little wrinkles had more to do with smiling than with age. Full, sensuous lips curved in a perpetual smile, like most people were around for his amusement. The only imperfection she found on his face was a tiny scar on his chin. That imperfection on a particularly perfect backdrop looked out of place.

She glanced back up into those mesmerizing eyes and saw a twinkle of humor. It was then Marlow realized she'd been sitting there, staring at him like a fourteen-year-old with a crush.

She cleared her throat.

"Well, I don't drink much coffee."

"Why not?"

"Mr. Jones——" she said, but he didn't let her finish.

"Jane, I really think that since I was hired to pleasure you, and you won't allow me that privilege, you should grant me one wish."

She glanced around, wondering whether or not the other patrons had heard the comment.

"What wish?"

"I would like you to call me by my first name."

"Okay." *Really, how much could it hurt?* "What's your first name?"

"Liam," he said.

"Liam. Unusual name."

"Named after my grandfather on my father's side of the family. Now, explain to me why you don't drink a lot of coffee."

"Oh, I like it with lots of cream and sugar." He smiled

and she remembered him silently watching her doctor her coffee. "I also have a stressful job. Caffeine is not a good thing to add to the mix."

"What kind of job do you have?" he asked as he sank back into the booth.

The tip of his boot nudged her ankle as he sprawled out, and she moved her feet a little to her right to give him room.

"I work in the family business. We're having a little trouble right now, and it's been a struggle keeping the stress down." That was an understatement. All the stress started building up, knotting her neck and left a stone weight in her belly. It seemed to have taken up residence there six months prior and had yet to break the lease. At least she'd finally convinced her father to hire a consultant.

"Must be hard to work so closely with your family."

Liam didn't touch her ankle again. He shifted slightly, and she tried not to notice the shuffling underneath the table. She really had no idea what he was doing down there, but she didn't have the nerve to ask him. Then she heard the thunk of his boot on the floor while his other foot hit the table, rocking it, causing a little of her coffee to spill onto the table.

She grabbed some napkins and cleaned the table. Before she looked up, though, his sock encased toe nudged her ankle. Slowly, she looked up from the table at him. From his lazy smile, she knew it hadn't been a mistake. The silk thigh highs she wore slid with his toe, slithering against her skin and wreaking havoc with her concentration.

"Jane?"

She looked at him, wondering what he wanted. When she didn't answer, his smile widened.

"Is it hard to work with your family?"

Oh, yeah, he had asked a question. She cleared her throat again.

"Sometimes." Her voice had taken on a husky edge she had rarely heard before.

"In what way?" he asked, still running his toe along the side of her ankle.

"Hmmm, oh, well, it's hard to get away from problems at work and enjoy time with the family."

"Ah, so part of celebrating your birthday was for you to relax."

"Yes. Joey worries," she said, trying to control her voice. Liam had moved his toe behind her ankle, sliding it up her calf.

"Joey, the woman who hired me?"

"Yes, Joey said I needed a break."

His eyelids were half closed, and his lazy smile had taken on a seductive edge. "Mr. Jones!"

"Mmmm?"

She attempted to move her feet to the left, over his feet, but as soon as she placed them back on the floor, he started to rub her right ankle. Slowly, he moved his toe around to the back of her ankle, following the same path up her calf that he had on her other leg. Warmth seeped into the pit of her belly with each brush of his warm foot.

Marlow's pulse hitched, and her nipples tightened against the lacy fabric of her bra as he continued to move his toe, slowly up and down the back of her leg. His eyelids had drooped so much, only a hint of his green eyes showed through the slits. His nostrils flared slightly, and she realized he was aroused.

"Mr. Jones——" she started, and his eyes opened slightly.

"You said you would call me Liam." He rose up from his slumped position.

She looked down at her clasped hands resting on the table. "I did, Mr. Jones, but——"

"Liam," he said, his voice taking on a slight edge.

She glanced up, and found a mixture of arousal and determination in those gorgeous green eyes.

"Liam," she said and watched him relax, sinking back against the back of the booth again. "I really don't think you understand, and I'm sure this," she said, nervously pointing her finger back and forth between the two of them, "might be second nature for you. But, really, you don't have to put on a show for me. I understand."

"You understand?" he asked, his voice neutral.

"Yes, I'm sure in your line of business, you're used to, well, must be forced, well..." She stopped, trying to keep herself from looking like a fool.

"Listen, Jane, whatever you're thinking, it's not because of the job."

"Oh," she said, feeling her face heat, "I'm sorry for the mistake."

His toe fell away and he sat up straight. "No, it's not a mistake. This," he said, angrily mimicking her movement with his hand between them, "has nothing to do with my job." He took hold of her hand and turned it so the palm faced up. "This has everything to do with chemistry."

"Chemistry?"

A shiver of excitement raced through her as his fingers slid sensuously in a circle over the palm of her hand. The heat that had invaded her belly now slid down between her legs. She shifted, trying to quell the searing inferno blazing through her system. It did no good.

"Chemistry. You and me." His voice deepened. "We have chemistry. What I can't understand is why you don't want to act on it."

"You find me attractive?"

He slowly nodded.

"You want to sleep with me?"

"Well, sleeping wasn't what I had in mind, Ms. Smith." His lips curved into a smile that promised he had more than one way to stay awake.

She shook her head. "Liam, I understand you may feel obligated to fulfill your contract. Really, I won't tell a soul."

He said nothing. He stood and walked around the table and sat down next to her. His eyes never left hers as he moved his fingers to the plump skin directly below her thumb. His spicy scent and heat surrounded her.

Up and down and around, again and again, he stroked the tender skin. Each caress tingled, all the way to the tips of her toes. Her heart beat wildly against her chest. Up, down, around. His eyes, dilated with arousal, totally focused on her. Up, down and around.

Still he said nothing.

"Liam," she said, half reprimand, half plea. Every fiber of her being was focused on his caress. Wet heat slid to her sex and her breasts ached.

"Jane, what's going on in that pretty little head?" he asked, his voice whisper soft. "Are you trying to come up with another idea to stall me?" He leaned closer, his lips almost touching her ear. "Or are you thinking about my fingers, hmm? Are you thinking what I could do with them, by chance?" His heated breath caressed her lobe, and she shivered.

"No." But she was now. His callused fingers continued their feather-light assault, and all she could think about was what it would feel like to have those fingers caress her breasts. She shifted again, and felt his lips curve a little bit more.

She found herself leaning closer to him. The temptation to lean against his shoulder, allow his body heat to seep into her, warm her from the inside out, almost overwhelmed her. She wanted to allow this man to run his fingers all over her body.

Marlow had fantasies, just like every average woman. But they were usually about celebrities, or nameless, faceless men.

Not any more.

Next to her sat six-foot-one of pure female fantasy. Trying to seduce *her*. With his golden brown hair, twinkling green eyes and dimples, he could charm an armadillo out of its hide.

Just like Vic. Vic, who had come to work for the company and charmed her into bed. Vic, who several weeks later, had told her he wanted nothing to do with her if she didn't help get him promoted.

Marlow jerked away from Liam, reminding herself of her promise: never let another man charm her and use her.

"Liam," she said, the husky desire still lingering in her voice, "I really don't think this is going to work. I'm just not interested."

"Jane," he chastised, "you're lying. I felt your pulse quicken. I bet your nipples are puckered so tight they hurt. You know you want me."

"I don't want to want you. That's what's important."

"Ah," he said, and he rubbed his thumb over the pulse on her wrist. "You don't want to want a man whom you control? Someone there for your pleasure? Does that scare you?" His eyes were now almost emerald green. "Jane, let me be yours for the evening. You tell me what gets you hot. *You* tell *me* what to do to you."

The thought of having a man at her command, who was schooled in the seductive arts, caused her heart to thump rapidly. She looked at that smile, his green eyes and knew this was a once in a lifetime chance. *She* would be the one in control of the situation. *She* would be the one calling the shots, directing the show. Excitement bubbled up at the thought of ordering this man to pleasure her. One night, no attachments. No way for her heart to get involved. Still…she wasn't into one-night-stands.

Then she thought about going back to her hotel room, sleeping in that big bed all by herself. All alone. No one to cuddle with. No one to kiss goodnight. She looked at Liam. *What would it be like to sleep next to him? To have him to spoon with, his arm draped over my stomach through the night. The very heat of him warming my back.* She wanted that. For this one night, she *deserved* that.

Marlow Jane Smith, a woman who always plotted and planned, a woman who left nothing to chance, never stepped out of her comfortable shell, ran as fast as she could and jumped off a cliff.

"Follow me to my hotel."

Chapter 2

After following little Miss Jane Smith to her hotel, Liam wondered why she invited him back to her room. She drove a plain beige sedan, stopped at every stop, and obeyed the speed limit. From her car to her personality, he was positive she never took a chance on anything. But, for whatever reason, she decided to break out of her mold tonight, and he was the lucky bastard who would reap the rewards.

He followed her through the lobby of her hotel, which, after seeing her car, surprised him. Situated close to The Galleria, it was one of the pricier hotels, even for this area. She hurried to the elevator, her heels clicking on the tile floor, echoed through the almost empty lobby. She punched the button, and then crossed her arms.

They waited a second or two, neither of them touching. For him, he knew as soon as he touched her soft skin again, he would have her naked and panting within five minutes. Images of her spread naked before him, breathlessly waiting for him to give her pleasure, caused all the blood to drain from his head into his groin. He shifted his feet, trying to ease the uncomfortable tightness of his jeans.

The elevator doors opened and a flock of women streamed out. They were laughing and one or two of them threw him a suggestive glance. He smiled at them as they passed and they broke into another round of giggles.

Jane walked into the elevator and punched the button to her floor. Liam had to jump through the doors before they closed on him.

"You know, you could act like we're together," he said, half-jokingly. The other half was irritated she was embarrassed to be seen with him.

"Well," she said, her smile sickly sweet, "so could you."

He would've come up with a stinger but her scent drove him insane. During the short walk from the club to the diner, her lavender scent, mixed with her own feminine musk, drifted behind her, licking at his senses. He lifted his hand to his nose, sniffing the vague remainder of her scent, like some bull in rut. He had to fight a raging hard-on since the moment they'd met and each time her scent reached him, he fought the overpowering need to stake his claim on this woman.

He stood far enough away from her to observe that curvy little body. The red dress accentuated her shape just enough. Although he loved bare midriffs and mini skirts, he always found more pleasure in unwrapping a package than in seeing its contents exposed. Her dress clung to those curves, but other than a hint of cleavage and a whole lot of leg, it kept secrets he couldn't wait to discover.

They reached her floor and he followed her to her room. Once inside, the enormity of the suite surprised him. All of this for little Ms. Jane Smith. As he surveyed the surroundings, she discarded her belongings and paced nervously, stopping to fidget with items throughout the room.

Worried she was having second thoughts, he sauntered up behind her. He inhaled her scent again.

"You know." She started at his voice and turned to face him. "It's normal to have second thoughts." Relief shone in her eyes, but before she could dismiss him, he continued. "But, not doing this would be a mistake, Jane. You want to do this. "

Liam took hold of her arm and pulled her close until their bodies touched. She stared at his neck. A slight flush warmed her cheeks and she kept her eyelids lowered. He surrounded her with his arms, pulling her body flush with his. Tightening his hold so her breasts flattened against his chest. He could feel her nipples practically stabbing him. He let loose a breath he hadn't realized he'd been holding.

He placed one finger underneath her chin and raised her face. The blue depths of her eyes shone with equal parts arousal and confusion. He lowered his head to take her lips in a slow, controlled kiss, when her little tongue darted out, licking the lower, plumper one. With a groan, he bent his head.

First, he nibbled on the lower lip, heat coursing through his body at the sweetness. She moaned and, abandoning his usual control, he devoured every inch of her luscious mouth. She hesitated for only a second, then threw her arms around his neck and returned the kiss with enthusiasm. Excitement surged through him. He slid his arms around her waist, pulling her body closer. She tried standing up on tiptoe to reach him better, so he cupped her cute little ass and lifted her. She moaned and wrapped her legs around his waist, grinding her mound against his cock. He almost dropped her when her heat reached him through the layers of their clothing. His fingers tightened on each cheek pulling another deep, aroused moan from her.

His tongue intruded past her lips, and Liam was surprised when hers boldly tangled with it. He tasted her sweetened coffee, along with a heady dose of her arousal. When he realized he was contemplating taking her up against the windows, he pulled back from the kiss. Both of them were breathing heavily. He gently lowered her to the floor. Her heartbeat pounded against her chest, beating in time with his. Liam pulled away from her, and took hold of her arm.

He steered her to the sofa in the living area. She sat down with a thump and avoided eye contact. He needed that contact. Her violet eyes were surrounded by a thick set of lashes and turned up at the corners, giving her an exotic look. Every time he looked at them, he lost his train of thought.

Liam sat down beside her.

"Jane," he said. She didn't respond. "Jane?"

Her head shot up and she finally made eye contact. Her eyes reflected every emotion she felt and right now, she was very wary.

"Oh," she said, as if she hadn't known she was sitting next to him.

"Why don't you sit back? That's right. Now, give me your foot."

She hesitated and then plopped her foot in his lap, killer heels and all, almost unmanning him. He slipped the shoe off, dropped it on the floor, and began to massage her foot. All the stiffness that had invaded her body when he had broken off their kiss, melted when his fingers gently rubbed her foot.

She closed her eyes and let loose a ragged moan. "Oh, that feels wonderful. I hate heels."

"Why don't you tell me why your friend thought you needed an escort for the evening? I've been trying to figure out why you'd need to pay some man for pleasure." He really couldn't. Jane was shy, but passion bubbled beneath that cool ivory skin. And, unless he missed the signs, she was on the verge of coming during their kiss.

He continued to knead her foot, giving special attention to her arch. She really had cute feet. They were small, with high arches, and each one of her little toes was painted red to match her dress.

"Jane?"

"Mmm, oh, well I'm..." She broke off as another moan escaped, this time in response to the pressure he applied to her arch. "I have a feeling I might be frigid."

He dropped her foot in his lap and laughed.

Her eyes flew open and her face flamed. She scrambled to get her foot out of his lap and stand up. Liam held onto it, preventing her from standing. Guilt sliced through him when he saw the hurt in her eyes before she dropped her gaze to her lap.

"Honey, look at me," he said gently. She lifted violet eyes. A shimmer of tears brightened them, and he felt like a heel. "The reason I laughed is because you couldn't possibly be frigid. Any woman who responds the way you did, is far from frigid. Jesus, all I'm doing is touching your feet. I know for a fact your panties are wet." Satisfaction swelled when she blushed and he knew he was right.

"Well, I never, you know," she said. She tried to pull her foot away from him, but he refused to relinquish it. He bent and grabbed the second one, taking off her shoe and throwing it on the floor.

"Now, why don't we talk about this problem you think you have?"

"I know I have a problem, Liam. I can't have an orgasm during sex."

He had to admire her honesty.

"Maybe your partners have been at fault. But you say you

can't have one during sex. Have you tried any other time?"

"Liam..." she said.

"What? How am I supposed to pleasure you if I don't know anything about you? That's impossible." He continued massaging and contemplated his next move. "I'm assuming from your comments, you've had more than one partner." He waited for her nod.

"I was even married for a few months when I was younger," she said quietly.

"And there have been several men since?" he asked, swallowing a sharp stab of jealousy. He didn't even know this woman and, for the first time in almost twenty years, he was jealous.

She nodded again. "Well, it's been three years. The last relationship really didn't go too well." She leaned back against the arm of the sofa again, closing her eyes and giving herself up to the massage. "He worked for our company. He'd moved into the area so I really didn't know him. You see my family's business is in a small town. Most of the people I've known my whole life."

Her voice had relaxed, and her Texas accent slipped in. He moved a little closer, unnoticed by Jane because she seemed lost in a memory. From the little frown, he figured it wasn't a good one. "Vic and I started dating and a couple months later we started sleeping together. It was...okay, I guess. Anyway, about three months later, he began hitting me up to put in a good word for him with my father. When I finally told him to stop hounding me, and then broke it off, he insinuated I was frigid. Since I'd never had an orgasm, I figured he was right. Liam, you're hurting my leg."

He looked down at his hand and realized he had her calf in

a death grip. He relaxed his hands.

"Sorry." He massaged away the sting.

Her lips curved into a closed mouth smile that reached down into his gut. Her eyes were still shut but the little humming noises she made sent a wave of heat spiraling through him.

He studied her, going over what little he knew about her. What kind of woman was little Ms. Jane? She followed the rules—she'd proven that. *Except when it comes to me.* He smiled.

"Tell me something, Jane, do you always follow the straight and narrow? From the way you dressed, I would have taken you for a real rebel."

A flush of red stained her ivory skin, from her breasts to the very top of her forehead. Seeing her skin flushed brought back the memory of his earlier fantasy. Jane lying amongst tangled sheets, her skin flushed with excitement, dewy with exertion, and the scent of her musky arousal filling his senses.

She cleared her throat, twice. "I've always done what my parents wanted. Well, except for the divorce. And, I'm not married with five children."

He moved his hand to her knee and gently caressed the tender skin behind it. Her eyes slid shut and she leaned her head back and purred. There was no other way to describe it. She sounded like a kitten with a bowl of the best cream. He pressed harder and she let out a shuddering sigh. Her tongue darted out and licked her full bottom lip.

"So," his voice was almost unrecognizable, "you must be close to your family if you work with them."

"Hmmm? Oh, yes, very close. I'm an only child. My father married late in life, and he still has some old-fashioned ideas. At least when it comes to me."

"So hiring a gigolo wouldn't be something he'd think fitting

for a young lady to do?" he asked, hoping she was loose enough
to joke about it. She let out a husky chuckle that vibrated down
his spine, almost bringing his painful state of arousal to an end.
The woman had to be crazy not to know just how sexy she
really was.

"Well, let's just say my father wouldn't think my sexual
satisfaction is very important. Bloodlines are very important to
Daddy."

He slid his hand up her thigh and found the lacy top of her
thigh high stockings. Caressing the sensitive skin just above the
lace had him so hard he was amazed he didn't come right there
in his pants. Liam was a man known for his control, both in and
out of the bedroom. He was also known for his ladies first policy. In an attempt to calm his pulse and his libido, he sucked in a
breath. Jane deserved better treatment.

He skimmed his hand up her thigh and his heart jumped
out of his chest when he felt curls instead of silk panties. They
were dewy with her arousal, wetting his fingers as he brushed
over them. Liam looked up when she shuddered.

"Ms. Smith," he admonished, arousal making his voice
hoarse, "I am surprised at you. I thought you were such a *good
girl.*"

Another shudder racked her system. His fingers stroked
over her curls once, twice...

"Liam..." she said, her voice a husky growl.

"Ms. Smith?"

"Liam, quit teasing me," she said, her voice catching as he
pressed her clitoris ever so slightly with his thumb. She raised
her hips to increase the pressure, but Liam removed his thumb
and continued the feather-light strokes.

"Now, Ms. Smith, you're going to have to tell me what

you need. Do you need this?" he asked, gliding one finger lightly against her folds. "Or," he said, caressing with his thumb again, "do you need this? You have to tell me, or," he removed his hand and settled it on her thigh, "I just might not be able to do my job."

"I liked what you did with your thumb."

"Ahhh." He returned his hand and gently pressed his thumb against her clit again. Ever so lightly, he shifted his thumb up, then down. "Is that what you want, Ms. Smith?"

"No, do it harder." Frustration dripped from her voice. He chuckled and pressed harder, up and around the area. Apparently, it still wasn't hard enough. She dropped one foot onto the ground and pushed her hips up, trying to increase the pressure. She gave a disgusted sigh. "Liam, do it harder."

He pressed his thumb against the tender skin as he slid one finger inside her. Slowly in and out. Her chest rose and fell with her short choppy breaths, and she licked her lips. Adding another finger, he increased his rhythm, satisfied when a long, ragged moan escaped from her. Using his thumb, he pressed with just enough force to send her hurtling over the edge. Spasms racked her body as she shattered, her mouth opened in a silent cry as her orgasm overtook her body.

Damn, she's beautiful.

Her juices drenched his hand; the musky scent drove him insane. The woman burned hotter and faster than a firecracker. Liam contemplated tasting her but decided he was too far-gone for that.

He knew he could make her come again. This time, he was going to be inside of that tight glove so he could feel her explode again.

He unbuttoned and unzipped his pants. He reached into

the back pocket of his jeans and retrieved his wallet, fumbling, but finally retrieving the condom. Ripping the foil packet open, he sheathed his cock, and pulled little Ms. Jane Smith across his lap. Her mound pressed against him, her wet heat almost sending him over the edge.

"Jane, honey," he pleaded.

She opened those beautiful eyes halfway, and gave him a satiated smile. Just that one little curving of her lips sent triumph speeding through him. Liam thought she might be too relaxed from her orgasm, until she slid her mound back and forth against his cock. He shuddered when her silken folds glided over his shaft.

Jesus, he would be lucky to make it three or four strokes. She looked down at him, confidence shining in her eyes, and mounted him without a word, sliding slowly down until he was in her to the hilt. Her inner muscles clenched around him, sending another roll of heat shooting through his system. Sweat beaded on his brow as he attempted to hold back, to draw out the pleasure for both of them.

Desperately, he tugged at the front of her dress, exposing a lacy bra. Without even admiring the lingerie, he unhooked the front closure. Her breasts sprang free, snowy white skin with nipples the color of raspberries. *So sweet.* He took one in his mouth, twirling his tongue around then sucking. His other hand caressed the other breast, bringing her nipple to a turgid peak. She repeated his name over and over. Each time she said it, the tension coiled tighter in his groin.

Jane rode him at such a slow pace he was ready to scream in frustration. He needed to come. He needed to come right then. Liam reached to grab her hips to set the pace, but she smacked them away. He tried the same move, so she took hold of each hand, holding them behind his head on the back of the couch, and continued to control the pace.

"Jane…" he said, trying to sound threatening but it came out almost as a groan when she gyrated her hips. She murmured his name and then she quickened her pace, increasing the speed with each stroke. The first tremors of her climax vibrated around him.

"Liam, yes!" she shouted, slamming down onto him, causing him to thrust into her hard. Her contractions pulled him further inside and milked his orgasm from him as he shouted her name.

She collapsed on top of him. His mind drifted for a few seconds. Every bone in his body seemed to have dissolved with his orgasm. She nibbled on his earlobe and he realized he must have dozed for a few seconds.

"Mmmm, Liam, you smell good."

He chuckled. "From my professional point of view, Ms. Smith, you are not frigid."

She laughed, the first completely carefree laugh he had heard. That playful laugh, filled with spent passion, and the feel of her inner muscles clasping his cock had him hardening again. Fast, even by his standards.

"Well, Mr. Jones, I think you just may be right. But I do have one request." Her tone had turned serious. And he looked up into her violet eyes sparkling down at him. "Next time, we *will* make it to the bed, and I want your clothes off."

Laughing, he jumped from the sofa, and headed to the bedroom, her legs wrapped around his waist, her silky stockings sliding against his skin.

"Round two, in the bedroom."

Her husky laughter filled the room.

* * * *

The first streams of light filtered through a small slit in the curtains. For a moment, Liam couldn't remember where he was. Then the memories flooded back—the club, Jane approaching him, convincing her to let him come to the hotel with her.

He rolled over, reaching for Jane and found an empty bed. He cracked open one eye and inhaled the scent of lavender, intermingled with the musky scent of passion. Closing his eyes, he relived the passion he and Jane had shared in that very bed the night before. Well, there, the couch, the shower, and even the desk chair. The woman surely got her money's worth, he thought with a smile. But the smile faded as he realized he never did explain the mix up to her.

"Jane, honey, come back here."

Silence answered him. "Jane?"

He jumped out of bed. Uncertainty gnawed at his stomach. Surely she wouldn't skip out on him. He thought about her reservations, her nervousness.

Hell, yes, she would!

"Jane!" he shouted, stomping through the suite. He grabbed the phone to call the desk when he saw the envelope with his name.

He dropped the receiver, picked up the envelope, and pulled out the note inside. A hundred dollar bill fell from it and landed on the desk. He unfolded it.

Liam,
Thank you for making my birthday so special.
Jane

Chapter 3

Liam's hand skimmed along Marlow's spine as she sat on top of him, riding him. Rivulets of water cascaded over them, making their skin slick. She moved faster, almost desperate to achieve the end, to release the tension building since the moment he touched her. His lips pulled at her nipple and she gasped as she felt the bite of his teeth. All the heat coiled in her belly broke free as spasms racked her body.

Marlow opened her eyes, her breath coming out in short gasps. She glanced around. Once again, she found herself daydreaming about that night in Dallas. The dampness in her panties made her squirm. Leaning back in her chair, she took a breath and studied the view of Abilene from her office, trying to gather her wits. Focusing on work, whether it was getting a report together, or paying attention to the conversation during meetings, had been difficult since she returned from her birthday weekend in Dallas.

Almost three months had passed, and she still couldn't get the man out of her mind. She would fight the memories, but inevitably, something someone said or did would remind her of that night. Before she could stop them, scenes from the hotel room would rush to the forefront of her mind, causing her to lose track of the present.

Just that morning, her father had called her name three times trying to get her to answer a question about the upcoming October promotions.

The worst part of it was the dreams. She would go to bed each night at ten o'clock and be awake by two, sweating and panting. Her nipples painfully tight, and she swore she felt his fingers as they glided over her skin.

When she realized she was sitting at her desk, during the middle of the day, swiveling her chair from one side to another, trying to rid herself of the ache between her thighs, she felt like an idiot. She took another breath, turned to face her desk, and started to study the information for her meeting with Ken.

Her door slammed open, and Joey rushed into her office. She was still a little irritated with Joey. When she confronted her the Monday after her birthday, Joey had said, "You needed to get laid."

Since she really couldn't argue with that, she let it go. Really, how could she complain about the most amazing sex she had ever had? *Or ever would have.*

"That consultant you father hired just walked down the hall, and oh, man. I would like to take a bite off that hunk."

Joey was never subtle when it came to men or sex. Or anything for that matter, especially the way she dressed.

Today she wore an electric blue dress that fitted snugly against the numerous curves of her killer body. It stopped mid-thigh, allowing for a great view of her shapely legs. She wore matching three-inch heels that gave her added height she really didn't need.

"Good looking?" Marlow asked, not particularly interested. No way could he be as good looking as Liam. Okay, so that sounded very junior highish, but the man had given her multiple orgasms.

"Yeah, he has…oh darn, here they come. Sit up straight and try to look sexy."

"Thanks, mom," Marlow said sarcastically. "Why do I need to look sexy?"

"Marlow, do you even plan on having decent sex again?"

"I'm going to dinner with Ken on Friday."

Joey snorted. "I said decent sex."

"Marlow, my girl," her father boomed from the doorway. She tried not to frown at his use of the word girl. "I want you to meet Liam Campbell."

Hammond Smith stood in her doorway, dwarfing her office. A big boned man, close to six-foot-five inches tall, with thick salt and pepper hair. She stood to greet him, and then shifted her gaze to the man who had followed her father through the door and now stood beside him.

Those green eyes, that dark blonde hair, that smile.

Oh, Lord.

The room tilted from one side to the other. Her knees threatened to give. Every thought in her mind halted, then catapulted. This could not be him. She gulped. *Good God, it was him.*

Liam stared at her. A little confusion clouded his sexy bedroom eyes. She took a deep breath and found her voice.

He walked forward and she extended her hand. "My pleasure, Mr. Campbell."

"I'm sure the pleasure is all mine, Ms. Smith." Both dimples appeared, and he held onto her hand, brushing his thumb across the crevice of skin between her thumb and forefinger. Little shivers of awareness radiated from that very spot. "And I'd be pleased if you would call me Liam."

"Yes," she said, amazed her voice was actually steady. Her heart thumped against her chest so hard, she was sure it would crack a bone. "And, I would be more comfortable if you would call me Marlow." Covering her hand with his other hand, he continued to caress her skin.

"Very unusual name." Sliding his fingers over the top of her hand left a trail of tingly skin in its wake.

"It was my mother's maiden name." She gave her hand a little jerk, finally breaking free of his hold. Her hand still tingled where he had caressed it with his fingers. There wasn't one ounce of comprehension in his eyes. Relief warred with irritation because he didn't seem to recognize her.

She motioned towards Joey. "This is my executive assistant, Joey Vernon. Joey, this is Liam Jo...Campbell."

Joey stepped forward, sexuality oozing out of every pore. She wasn't a woman who did it on purpose, it was just the way she was. She would smile at a man, and he would forget his mother's last name.

Liam studied Joey from head to toe and back up again. It was a long study because Joey was almost five-foot-nine without the three-inch heels she wore. If you factored in her Texas-sized blonde curls, she was well over six feet.

"Nice to meet you, Ms. Vernon," he said shaking her hand and then releasing it. He turned his sea-green gaze back to Marlow. Joey turned and looked at Marlow, arching one perfectly sculpted eyebrow.

"Now that you've meet the girls," her father said, and Liam smiled slightly when she cringed at her father's use of that word again, "we'll go look over those plans you have for me. Marlow, we're doing lunch. Meet us in the lobby around noon."

"Once again, Marlow, it was a pleasure." Marlow shivered

as Liam's Texan accent rolled over the word pleasure.

"He was totally into you," Joey gasped as soon as the door closed. "I mean, he took a look at me," she said, her hands motioning up and down her body, "all men do, but, well, he wants you."

Marlow collapsed into her chair and dropped her head on her desk with a thud.

"I'm going to hell," she said morosely. "That or I was some kind of monster in another life, and this is the payback."

Joey perched her hind end on the edge of Marlow's desk. "No, hon, you are not going to hell because one of the hottest guys I've ever seen is into you. Did you see the size of his hands? I wonder if he's proportional, if you know what I mean?"

"He is," she said, but realized that Joey didn't react due to her voice being muffled with her head facedown on her desk. She lifted her head, and set her chin on her fisted hands. "He is."

Joey's whiskey brown eyes widened and her mouth opened and closed, twice. For the first time in four years, Marlow saw her at a loss for words.

"He's the guy."

"The guy?" A frown marred Joey's perfect beauty.

"The guy, the guy you hired!" Marlow's voice edged towards hysteria.

"Oh my God! He's your gigolo?" she screeched.

Marlow stood and nervously paced the area between her desk and her window. "Why don't you take an ad out in the ABILENE REPORTER, Joey? I'm not sure they heard you over in Wylie."

"But, you knew this guy's name, didn't it click?" she asked.

"No, he used a different last name."

"Well, the guy I hired was named Jim Jones."

"Jim Jones? Jim Jones?" She looked at Joey, wondering if she would have to explain. She saw nothing but confusion in her eyes. "You hired a gigolo for me with the same name of the man who poisoned hundreds of people in the name of religion?"

"Oh," she said, comprehension in her eyes. "I didn't even think about that. Well, anyway, *this* is the guy you slept with." She shrugged. "Big deal."

"Joey," she said through clenched teeth, "it *is* a big deal. This one knows I paid a man to have sex with me."

"You didn't pay him, I did. And I'm sure he didn't get the money. Jim did."

She closed her eyes and counted to ten. Joey was a genius at office management, but she had a laid back attitude towards sex, something Marlow usually admired and envied. At the moment, though, it irritated her.

"I left him an extra hundred in the morning."

"Ohhh, he must have been good." Marlow's face heated and Joey laughed. "So, let me get this straight. He used his real name?"

"No, I mean he used his first name. I called him Mr. Jones first so that's where the mix up actually happened. In fact, now that I think back on it, he insisted on using his first name. I used my middle name. That's why I know he didn't recognize me."

"Don't be ridiculous. From the way he looked at you, he must have recognized you."

"No, he looks that way at every woman. Men like him flirt with anything that moves and they think they know what we all look like naked."

"Well, it's true in your case."

"Shut up." She pointed at Joey. "This is all your fault. You hired the man. At least he doesn't recognize me." When Joey looked as if she would protest what Marlow said, "Look at the way I'm dressed now and think about what I looked like that night in Dallas."

Joey studied her and Marlow knew what she saw. Grey shapeless suit, no makeup, thick glasses, long black hair pulled into a tight bun at the nape of her neck. The only jewelry she wore was a cameo, left to her by her grandmother, pinned to the collar of her blouse.

"I disagree with you. He barely glanced at me, which, when you think about it, is strange. And, it's only a matter of time, Marlow. You may not dress like you did that night, but your eyes are very distinctive. Even if you hide them behind those hideous glasses."

Marlow's knees gave way, and she sat down with a thud. She sighed, wondering if she could manage to wear her sunglasses through lunch.

* * * *

Marlow's father, Ham, had chosen Joe Allen's BBQ for lunch. Situated on an industrial road, it was housed in several buildings that looked fused together. The interior was a little dark, and the floor was uneven in several places, but Liam liked places with atmosphere, and the food was beyond description.

As Ham droned on about Abilene's assets, Liam held onto his temper. He still couldn't believe that little Ms. Jane was actually Ham Smith's daughter. At first, he hadn't recognized her. She had scraped her glorious hair back in to a tight, controlled knot. The suit she was wearing looked like it was made for a prison matron, hiding any curves she possessed. She was also wearing glasses today. So, at first, he hadn't paid much attention to Ham Smith's little girl.

Then she spoke. Cool and controlled, not one sign of recognition in her voice. It didn't matter. He would know that voice anywhere. It haunted his dreams. The memory of her moans kept him up at night and ruined his concentration during the day. Because of some five-foot-two sexual dynamo, he had cancelled dates and stopped pursuing women altogether. And there she sat. Acting as if she had never met him, acting as if he had never swallowed her cries when she came. He shifted, trying to ease the semi-hard-on he sported whenever she was near.

He glanced in Marlow's direction, and she averted her eyes again. She recognized him. He would bet his life on it. Apparently, she found the table more interesting to study than talking to him. He nodded when Ham asked him a question, not really hearing what he agreed to.

He knew she was embarrassed. It didn't mean he excused her behavior. How could she think she was going to get away with acting like she didn't know him? He had news for her. She wasn't. Little Ms. Marlow had a lot of questions to answer.

What was it about the woman that drove him insane? It wasn't the never-ending instructions she gave when she ordered her food. The woman gave more directions on how to cook her food than a brain surgeon needed for surgery. Women with that many rules tended to be complicated. He didn't like complications.

It definitely was *not* her plain suit or quiet nature. Although he loved everything about women, even the quiet ones, he was usually attracted to outgoing personalities. He didn't always date women who were considered beautiful, but they usually matched his flirtatious nature. Like Joey, the executive assistant, who apparently knew how to buy men for her friends. Yeah, he remembered her name also. One night with this woman, who paid him a hundred dollars for his time, had him sitting home Saturday nights, avoiding women he knew were looking for a good time. It had gotten so bad that Heath was worried about him.

And, until today, he couldn't really remember what she looked like. He remembered gliding his hand through her hair, along her body. But all that was left of that night were slivers of memory and the sound of her moans. Until he walked into her office today, and Marlow opened her mouth and said his name. He shuddered, remembering the way her voice sounded when she said his name. He was irritated, mad, and downright frustrated.

Usually, women were a joy for him. He loved to flirt with them, work with them and he definitely loved to make love to them. Each woman, young, or old, tall or short, thin or pleasantly rounded, had her own unique personality. Their smiles, their scent, even the way they brushed their hair mesmerized Liam. And, although he was well known to be a ladies' man, he counted more ex-lovers as friends than any man he knew. He always kept it light, and could charm any woman he knew, including his mother. For some unknown reason, he had felt a connection to Marlow the instant their hands touched.

When he took Marlow Smith's hand in his, tiny tremors zinged along his skin. He noticed her eyes, almost too big for her little face, widen behind her thick glasses and her lips part in a silent gasp. He had been glad he wasn't the only one who felt the awareness that shimmered between the two of them.

And there she sat, across the table next to her father, barely saying a word to him.

"Well, I guess you two will want to take off," Ham said.

He switched his gaze from Marlow, who had finally lifted her head from her study of the table. "Take off?"

"Yes, to look at some of the stores here in town. Marlow here can take you since she drove her own car."

He glanced over at Marlow and saw sheer panic in her eyes.

"Daddy," she said, and he could tell she was getting mad because her voice dipped an octave lower and a hint of Texas warmed her usually cool tone. "I have a lot of work to do today. I'm sure that Mr. Jo...er, Liam would like to get settled."

"Not much to settle Marlow, although I do appreciate the thought. I plan on jumping back and forth between here and Dallas." He turned his attention to her father. "Lately, a lot of our work has been in south Texas and southern Louisiana. Being this close will allow me to run back and forth between here and Dallas. I also plan on making a few trips up to Henrietta. My folks retired there on a piece of land." He saw immediate admiration in Ham's eyes. He turned to smirk at Marlow and swallowed a laugh when she scowled.

"Well, there you go. Besides, anything you have to do can wait until tomorrow, Marlow," Ham declared.

Liam hadn't turned his attention away from Marlow and saw her flinch when Ham made his ignorant statement. Marlow may have gotten her job because she was the owner's daughter but he could tell she took that job seriously. He didn't know her well but there was a strong strain of commitment that oozed from her. He smiled as he remembered how she approached him in the club, intent on breaking off her appointment.

He had been unsuccessful in finding out her real name, or anything else about her. After bothering a very cute desk clerk for thirty minutes, he'd come no closer to finding out Jane's true identity or where she was from. But, he had to agree with the desk clerk when she told him he should have found out the woman's name before he fell asleep. So, little Ms. Jane Smith had remained a mystery.

Until today.

Until Marlow Smith opened her mouth and welcomed him to Abilene.

On top of all of that, her whole demeanor during lunch had irritated him. She never voiced her opinion. Not once did saucy little Jane pop up. She allowed her father to guide the conversation, never once contradicting him, although she wanted to. Marlow, in her ugly gray suit, was buttoned down and boring. This wasn't the same woman who approached him in the bar.

Marlow stood and he followed her out, trying to reach the door before it slammed in his face. He stepped out and dry hot wind slapped his face. Ham walked up beside him, clapped his hand on Liam's shoulder, and chuckled.

"She's a good girl," her oblivious father said, "and she's one of the best to show you around a store. She's worked all four we have here in Abilene."

He shook her father's hand and then hurried to get to the car before Marlow decided to leave him. Irritation burst through him. The woman was always trying to leave him behind!

Her hands were gripping the wheel so tight that her knuckles were white.

"I really appreciate you doing this, Marlow," he said, throwing her his best smile, which was totally wasted because she threw the car in reverse and was busy looking out the back window. "I like to get the feel of a business, especially when I'm working with retail."

She pulled out onto the access road and headed in the op-posite direction from her office. The silence in the car hung heavily. He shifted in his seat and looked at the passing scenery. Finding nothing of interest, he turned his attention back to Mar-low.

"So why don't you tell me why you think Campbell Con-sulting can help you?" he asked, trying to keep some kind of conversation going. Now that he had her alone, he really didn't know how to confront her.

"Well, we need some help updating the stores, new ad campaigns."

"But there are other businesses you could have picked, and with your family money, could have afforded."

"True and all I did was recommend you. Daddy had the fi-nal choice." She flipped her turn signal and turned right. "But I looked at your record. The companies you work with aren't torn apart and put back together. You have to understand, a lot of the people who work for us are second and third generation employees. And although most business experts would say it was a mistake, we are family. I want to make Smith's better, but not at the expense of our employees."

He studied her for a second, and then turned to look out the window again. His mind bounced from one thought to the next. *Did she know I was the Liam from Dallas when she suggested they hire them?*

He thought back to her reaction when they were intro-duced. She had licked her lips and offered her hand. But her eyes told him exactly how she felt. He had seen a flash of panic before she could control it. No, she'd had no idea.

"Not a lot of upper management types care about the peo-ple who work at their stores, just their profit margin."

"That may be, but not for us. It's one of the things that we pride ourselves on. Everyone in the family has worked at the stores, even Mummy." Her lips curved into a secret smile. "Most of the people who work in management have worked in the stores, including me. These people are not numbers to us, Liam. They're family," she stated, a sliver of warmth invaded her usually cool tone.

She stopped at a red light, and he turned to take in her profile. Her black hair was pulled back into a tight little bun at the nape of her neck. It contrasted with her alabaster ivory skin and those full, red lips. He looked closely at her skin and realized she wore no makeup. Tortoise shell glasses, a little too big for her face, perched on her little upturned nose.

Even though he remembered her as a small woman, he had forgotten just how tiny she was. He tried to angle his head to see if she could actually reach the pedals on the floor.

She turned to look at him, because the leather creaked as he leaned in her direction in order to see her feet.

"Is there something wrong, Liam?" She looked at him as if he had lost his mind.

"Uh, no. Nothing." *Okay, that was slick.* What the hell was wrong with him?

She continued to stare at him. A shiver of heated recognition in those baby blues flashed, and he knew she remembered something from that night. The moment was ruined though, because the light turned green, and the car behind them honked. They jerked away from each other like two teenagers caught necking in the car.

She concentrated on her driving, never taking her eyes off the road. He took a deep breath and inhaled the scent of lavender. That scent skipped across his senses, teasing him, arousing him. The memories tumbled, one on top of the other. The feel of her ivory skin, her wet lips on his body, the smell of her lavender-scented skin intermingling with the musk of their passion.

He looked at Marlow again, taking in her delicate stature, her dark as midnight hair, those lips, and that overbite.

"Tell me, *Marlow*, you the only child?" he asked, satisfied when her fingers tightened around the steering wheel. "I mean, your father didn't mention any other children."

"No, just me," she said, her voice as cool as ice.

He shifted again, trying to get comfortable. That voice of hers shouldn't turn him on, but it did. Most people would probably hear it and think she was a frigid woman. Liam knew that cool exterior hid a very warm, very passionate interior. Every time he heard her voice, he remembered her moaning with her head thrown back, her hair wild around her shoulders. And every time he remembered that, his pants grew uncomfortably tight.

Should he come right out and ask her just what the hell she thought she was doing? Knowing Marlow, the broom handle would stiffen in her back and she would clam up.

He decided to take the indirect approach.

"Marlow, are you busy Friday night?"

Chapter 4

Marlow's breath caught in her throat and she choked before she could answer Liam. She glanced at him. He was smiling at her but she could swear she saw a bit of temper in his eyes.

She cleared her throat, trying to regain her composure. "I'm busy this Friday, but thank you for asking."

His eyes first widened in surprise and then narrowed. The silence hung again, and he continued to study her. She flipped the turn signal and turned into a parking lot of one of her father's grocery stores. Marlow sighed, relieved to be able to park the car and escape his scrutiny.

The parking lot of the store wasn't even half full, even though it was the middle of the day, once again reminding her of the trouble with sales.

Marlow hurried to the front door, knowing he was following her. The automatic door opened with a whoosh, bringing a flood of air-conditioned air with it. Sweat that had gathered at the nape of her neck slid down her back and caused her to shiver as the cold air surrounded her, chilling her skin.

Although it was one of their oldest stores and a bit outdated, this was her favorite. When she started working at the age of sixteen, Mr. Chambers, the former manager, took her under his wing, and treated her like every other kid working in the store. He took one look at the skinny little boss's daughter, and told her she had to pull her own weight. He had shown her the ropes of running a grocery store, giving her a respect for the people who worked in them.

Marlow hurried down the chip aisle, stopping to rearrange bags that were out of place. When she realized Liam was gaining on her, she headed to the storeroom.

Liam grabbed hold of her arm, stopping her. "I thought you said you were going to show me around."

She glanced at him and saw those two dimples and a flirtatious glint in his eyes.

"I will. But I wanted to say hi to someone. If you want to walk around and get a feel for the store, I can catch up to you," she suggested, hoping he would go away, somehow knowing she really didn't want him to.

Those dimples diminished ever so slightly, and he crossed his arms across his chest. "You know, I get the impression that you really don't like me."

Not like him? She was trying to divert her attention from him by visiting with Mr. Chambers. If she didn't do something, and do it quickly, she was afraid of exposing herself to him. Heat crept up her face as she thought of exposing herself to him in a totally different way.

"No, Liam, I like you. I just know to be wary of men like you." She once again attempted to escape to the storeroom.

He trailed behind her. "Men like me?"

They passed a group of twenty-somethings, and he smiled, causing a stream of giggling from them. She stood and watched as all of them dissolved like butter on the hot Texas pavement. Marlow looked at him, then at the women and rolled her eyes.

"You're a flirt," she said, and was equal parts relieved and saddened to see his smile fade. "I really don't think you're even aware you're doing it. It's second nature, but you are a flirt. And," she said, turning around and continuing her quest, "I'm not used to men flirting with me. It just makes me a little uneasy."

Marlow tried her best to ignore the jealousy and irritation burning a hole in her stomach. She glanced at him to see a look of astonishment cross his face. Marlow admonished herself. She was falling into the pattern of exposing her soul to him. He really was one of the easiest men to talk to.

Finally, they reached the storeroom, and she pushed through the doors and searched for Mr. Chambers. She found him reorganizing the area where they kept cereal. At the age of seventy-four, Mr. Chambers was still a fit man. Sure, he had to wear bifocals now, he had lost most of his hair, and he had a little paunch, but his light blue eyes still sparkled with mischief. He retired four years earlier and worked part-time managing the vendors.

He must have heard the click of her heels because he turned, irritation evident in his eyes until he saw whom it was. A genuine smile broke out on his face as he set down his clipboard.

"Mr. Chambers, how are you doing today?"

"I'm fine, just fine, Marlow." He looked over her shoulder and must have seen Liam. "So who is this fine young man you have with you? Another suitor?"

She laughed, knowing he was only kidding her. He knew

of the arguments she had with her father over the issue of marriage and usually introduced her to every new stock boy they hired as a joke.

"No. And stop that," she admonished. "It was bad enough that boy you hired last week almost passed out when you introduced me to him. Liam, I would like to introduce Mr. Sam Chambers. He trained me and has worked for Smith's longer than anyone else."

Liam stepped forward and shook his hand. "It's a pleasure to meet you, Mr. Chambers."

"Liam is the consultant we hired to help revamp the stores."

"Revamp the stores," he said, disgust lacing his voice. "You know what your father needs to do. He needs to fire the appliance and make you CEO." It was a familiar argument. One she heard each time the subject came up.

"Quit calling Ken an appliance. You could get fired," she said in a teasing voice.

"Can't help it, the boy's stupid," he said shaking his head. "Ken Moore, what a stupid name. Sounds like he should be on sale at Sears."

She could see Liam didn't bother to hide his smile and knew then he had met their newly hired CEO.

"Anyway," she said trying to change the subject, "Daddy wanted me to show Liam around, and I thought I should come around and check on you."

He smiled and then turned to Liam. "So, is Ms. Marlow Jane giving you the grand tour?"

The breath of air Marlow inhaled stuck in her throat, causing her to cough. Marlow dared not look in Liam's direction while the silence stretched out for a few uncomfortable seconds. She heard him shift from foot to foot, then cross his arms.

"Ms. Marlow *Jane* is showing me the ropes today. Even took me to Joe Allen's and *paid* for me."

"Yeah, well Ms. Marlow Jane is the heart and soul of this company."

"Mr. Chambers, you know that isn't true. I just handle promotions." She still hadn't looked in Liam's direction. Anxiety jangled along her nerves as she fought to control her outward reaction until she could escape.

"Don't listen to her, young man. She keeps this place going."

"Yes, well, we need to get going. Liam hasn't been to his hotel yet, and I'm sure he's ready to settle in."

"It was nice to meet you, Mr. Chambers." She still had not looked in his direction, and headed for the doors. Maybe she could make it to the car before he noticed she was gone. The minute his strong fingers wrapped around her elbow, she knew her hope was futile.

"Where are you rushing off to, Ms. Marlow *Jane?*" he asked. "We haven't been able to have a look at the store."

Instead of making eye contact, she concentrated on his Adam's apple but knew she would have to face him sooner or later. Slowly, she raised her eyes, first to his clenched jaw, then to his sensuous mouth now set into a grim line, and then she looked into his eyes.

His sea green eyes were not smiling down at her. They were narrowed, suspicion sparking with anger in them.

"Maybe we should go some place a little more quiet to discuss this," he said, his voice hard with determination. She bristled at the autocratic tone.

Marlow wrenched her arm free. "There is nothing to discuss, Mr. *Campbell*. " He had the good grace to wince and soften his stance, just a bit.

"Are you going to pretend you didn't recognize me?" he asked incredulously. People around them had noticed his tone and his raised voice and glanced in her direction. She cringed, thinking of the reports that would inevitably make it back to her father.

Deciding righteous indignation was the only way to get out of the argument, she stepped closer.

"Of course I recognized *you*. I just don't think there's any reason to discuss it." With that, she turned on her heel and headed to the produce section.

As she walked down the aisles, stock-boys, cashiers on their breaks, and vendors smiled at her. Liam watched as she returned their smiles and waves, knowing just how embarrassed and angry she was. He was sure it had to do with the manners drummed into her. The same damn manners that had landed her in his lap in the first place. If she didn't think she needed to apologize, she would never have mistaken him for her gigolo.

Liam followed her to the produce section. He saw her in the back, standing next to the onion bin, talking to a rather short, stocky man. He was dressed in the store uniform, so he guessed she was talking business. Deciding that confronting her was not the best thing to do, he strolled around the department.

He realized, although the variety he would have wanted wasn't there, it was clean and well kept. A mother was shopping, looking over the tomatoes, while her three-year-old stared at Liam with big blue eyes. She was really cute with her curly black hair and a smile that would slay men when she grew up. He returned her smile and she giggled.

"I don't think a woman in Abilene is safe from you and your dimples."

He turned. Marlow stood next to the vegetable rack, her arms crossed beneath her breasts.

"Really? I would think you determined me resistible since you left without leaving your name."

She sighed. "Why would I leave my name? Considering what I thought our relationship was."

Deciding that going over the whole big mess right now was not a good idea he tried to divert her attention.

"You worked produce, Marlow?"

She looked a little startled by the change in subject. "Yes, I've worked every department. I was even produce manager for awhile at an HEB in Austin."

She sounded disgruntled by the question. "Not your favorite department?"

"Ick." She turned and busied herself rearranging the cucumber pile. "I would come home smelling like produce." She picked up a cucumber, tested its firmness, and set it aside. "No matter how many times I washed my hands, I could still smell the onions."

She continued to pick up cucumbers, encircling them with her delicate hand, squeezing just a tad, then setting them down. Thinking about her soft hand, encircling him, squeezing him, testing for firmness, sent a curl of heat to his groin. He cleared his throat, hoping to change the subject.

"You know, I used to hate doing this. It was such a pain. At least with other things like meat, there was a date. These you had to sort through the rack, testing them, making sure they were firm enough to keep."

Throughout her comments, she continued picking up cucumbers, sliding her fingers around them, and applying pressure. He stood, mesmerized by her motions, remembering how she had slid her hand down his abdomen, taking his cock in her hand, her thumb just grazing over the tip. Never breaking eye contact, she had slid her thumb, back and forth, spreading the drop of liquid around the tip.

"You really know how to do your job well, Marlow."

His voice was rough. She glanced up, her eyes widening.

"You know just how much pressure to use." He stepped closer as she stood seemingly frozen by his comments. "If you apply too much pressure, you could have a disaster on your hands. Juice all over the place." She continued to stare at him. He stepped closer. Her eyes shimmered with the same hunger that gnawed at his gut. "But you, Marlow, you know just how to squeeze." She swallowed, and he could see the pulse flutter in her throat. He knew it! She still wanted him. "Of course, you have to finish what you started." He glanced down at his obvious erection. Quickly she lowered her eyes to his crotch, and it felt like a lick. She dropped the cucumber back in the rack and backed away from him.

"We...we have to get back, I mean I..." Her eyes dipped down again and back up, her face flushed. "I really have to get back." He saw determination harden her eyes. "I don't have time to play around, Liam."

She turned on her heel and all but ran for the exit.

He took several deep breaths, trying to bring himself under control. Jesus, he just meant to tease her, not get himself so hard it was painful to walk. One more gulp of air and the heat receded a bit and he followed her to the car. He grasped for something, anything to calm him down. Thinking about her reaction to him when he confronted her, caused his hormones to settle.

Irritation replaced arousal as he thought about the fact she hadn't intended to say anything to him. Marlow had planned on pretending she had never met him. *She* was angry with him. He was the one who'd been duped. After one of the most sexually satisfying nights of his life, if not the most, she walked out, not even leaving a number or address!

She knew who he was from the moment he stepped into her office. Now he thought about it, a spark of recognition flashed in her eyes when he had first made eye contact. Then, she never even let on that she was the woman who had been haunting his dreams for the last three months. She had even snuck into his daytime hours, bothering him with the memory of the sound of her sighs and the scent of her skin. She had some nerve thinking she had been wronged, just because he didn't recognize her.

The thought made him pause. He stood by the passenger side door and realized she did have some right to be a little mad. Just because he didn't recognize her at first, didn't make him a horrible person, but he definitely lost some points with her on that one.

He opened the door, sat down, and began to think about their situation. She slid the car into reverse and backed out of the space. Knowing he needed to get his mind off of her for a few minutes, he studied the surroundings. He noted a few potholes in the parking lot, but it was kept relatively clean, and there were no shopping carts around. The blue sign looked about ten years out of date and he was sure, come dusk at least one or two of the letters wouldn't light up. Smith's was one of the few remaining grocery chains that believed in baggers who not only bagged the groceries, but brought them to your car.

"I'm going to trust that you keep this mistake a secret," she said, her cool un-Texan like voice had returned.

"Oh," he said, carefully wading through the emotions she stirred, "and why would I do that?"

She had stopped at a light and turned to look at him, studying him as if he was a specimen in a lab. "However my father feels about me sleeping with a gigolo, you can be damn sure he wouldn't be happy having one revamping our company. Especially one who slept with his daughter under false pretenses."

The light turned green and she drove forward. He allowed her about thirty seconds to think she had the upper hand in the matter. Really, she thought he would allow her to walk away from him, just like that. There was no way he could spend the next few weeks working with her and not get another taste of her. She was going to give into him, one way or another. And it could start this week, even if she was busy Friday night.

He scowled and asked without thinking, "Who the hell are you going out with on Friday night?" Possessiveness dripped from his voice.

Her spine stiffened slightly but her voice was cool and controlled. "Not that it's any of your business, but I'm going out with Ken Moore."

She turned down the street that led to their headquarters' offices. His mind raced through all he knew about her and Moore.

"You're going out with the appliance? Let me guess, this

is a candidate for Mr. Marlow Smith?" He couldn't help the mocking tone that had invaded his usually flirtatious voice. *What the hell was it with this woman?* One minute he sounded like a jealous boyfriend, and the next he sounded like a three-year-old.

"Liam, you really have to believe me. I had no idea who you were. I think it best we just forget it ever happened."

"So, you just think I'm supposed to forget what had to be the best sex I've ever had in my life?"

She looked at him, opening and closing her mouth twice. "The best sex?" Her tone told him she didn't believe him.

"Yeah, definitely ranks in the top two or three, definitely." He crossed his arms over his chest. Great now he sounded like Rain Man.

"Top two or three?" she asked.

Her face was averted as she drove so he leaned forward to get a better look. Her knuckles were white from gripping the steering wheel. He sat back, trying hard not to chuckle. So, the little lady didn't like being compared to anyone else.

He studied her for a moment more and realized her borderline type A personality might help him win her over, if he put his knowledge to good use.

"Well,"—he paused for emphasis—"at least in the top ten."

He watched her little spine straighten even more and was amazed it didn't snap in half. She flipped the turn signal, and he realized they were turning into the parking lot of their offices. She pulled in next to his convertible Mustang and turned off the engine. Without a word, she grabbed her purse off the floor of her car, pushed open the door, and then slammed it behind her.

Yes, sir, she really didn't like him comparing her to other women. Maybe, just maybe, he could get her attention with the idea of competition. One thing was for sure; he wouldn't allow someone like Moore to touch her. He planned to do everything in his power to make sure Moore understood Marlow was off limits.

Chapter 5

Marlow hurried down the hall, hoping to get to the sanctuary of her office before Liam caught up with her. Joey wasn't at her desk when she breezed through the outer office. She slammed the door shut, leaned up against it, closed her eyes, and sighed.

"Marlow?"

Her eyes shot open, and she jumped when she saw Ken standing by the window, staring at her as if she had lost her mind. *Jeez, what the heck was he doing here?* He was the second to last person she wanted to see at the moment. Then she remembered he'd wanted to meet with her to review the Halloween promotions they had to get ready. Preparing for the holiday when it was as hot as Hades outside, didn't appeal to her.

With a resigned sigh, she released the doorknob and walked to her desk.

"Oh, nothing. Did you get my email about the problems we're having with that one vendor?"

"Yes, and truthfully, if he can't deliver what we need, we'll talk to the company," he said with a shrug.

Marlow studied her father's handpicked CEO. He was attractive in a corporate sort of way. A little under six feet, he kept his black hair cut short. Ken dressed well, always without a wrinkle in his suit. She really wished she could like him better, but there was something about him that was just so blah. She sighed again, causing Ken to look up from the report he was reading.

"I thought we were supposed to meet in your office, Ken."

"Your father said you were running a little late today because you were showing Campbell around. I just thought it would be easier on you to have the meeting here."

"Mmmm," she murmured, thinking about Liam, which was a dangerous thing to do. When she thought about him, she thought about those green eyes, those dimples, and those hands. His hands had touched every part of her body. Then she thought about touching every part of his body and the way she had glided her hands over his copper nipples, down his abs and wrapped her hand around his hard...

"Marlow?"

"Oh." Noticing the questioning look on Ken's face, she began feeling heat creep up her neck and then her face. *Good Lord!* She was turning into a sex maniac. "What were you saying?"

"Not much, just that I was looking forward to Friday night."

Her face burned hotter, but from shame, not embarrassment. Personally, she really liked Ken. Although blah, he was smart, and he loved to discuss everything from politics to movies. He was pleasant to be around, one of the reasons she had accepted his offer of dinner and a movie. The other reason she left sitting in her car.

She smiled. "I am, too. There's that new romantic comedy out I'd love to see."

"That sounds great," he said with a relieved sigh. "Now, back to the problems with the vendor."

Marlow settled back in her chair and stifled an urge to bolt.

* * * *

Liam sat in Marlow's car and thought about what to do. Mentally, he reviewed the facts and planned an attack. One, she didn't like hearing about the competition. That was very promising. Two, she couldn't hide her reaction to him and, if she had been telling the truth, she'd never been sexually satisfied until she met him. He snorted at the memory of her confession of being frigid.

A bead of sweat rolled down the side of his face, and he realized he was sitting in a closed car. Shaking his head, he stepped out of the car, just to be slapped in the face with a wave of heat. He shoved his hands into his pockets and followed Marlow into the building.

He had noticed, when Ham showed him around, the office was neat, clean and the people who worked there seemed to enjoy their jobs. One of the reasons both Liam and his brother, Heath, had wanted to work in consulting, was to work with companies like Smith's. But not the way most consultants did.

Most came in, gutted the company, and then left without a thought as to what they had done. That's what happened to both of his parents, who had worked for a wrapping paper manufacturer in Ft Worth. His parents had been lucky they'd worked for the company long enough to retire with their pensions. But so many of the people they knew hadn't. Many families lost their homes, along with their pensions, and moved out of the area to find work. Heath and Liam knew they could start a company to save family businesses like that and save the jobs.

He turned into the offices that led directly to Marlow's. People smiled and waved to him as he made his way through the collection of desks. Unlike other businesses, the floor plan of these offices didn't include cubicles. It was open, allowing for conversation to flow freely amongst the workers.

He reached the outer area that led to Marlow's office. Joey, his employer in a roundabout way, smiled at him when he walked through the door.

She let out a wolf whistle while she perused him from his head to his toes, then all the way back up again.

"You were worth every penny. And, I bet you were worth every dollar of that hundred dollar tip."

The tips of his ears burned, and he knew, for the first time since the age of eleven, he was blushing. Liam cleared his throat, and she laughed again.

"Hey, I'm just glad she finally let loose. But, if you're coming to see her, you have to wait in line. Ken had a meeting with her this afternoon, and he's in there with her."

"I take it from your tone that you don't like the guy." He propped his hip up on her desk.

"Ugh!" She leaned back in her chair and crossed her arms over a very exquisite chest. He looked at the woman most men would label gorgeous. From her big blonde hair, to those brown eyes, to the knockout hourglass figure showcased in an electric blue dress, the woman had the body and personality of a showgirl. *Usually my type of woman.* The funny thing was, he wasn't at all interested in her. He was only interested in what she knew about Marlow. "Don't get me wrong. He really seems like a nice guy, but Marlow doesn't need a nice guy. She needs someone like you."

Feeling a little put out by her assumptions, he said, "You don't think I'm a nice guy?"

She rolled her eyes and let out an exasperated sigh. "Personality wise you're great, although maybe a little too much of a flirt for Marlow. But, nice guys play by the rules and what Marlow needs is a rule breaker." She studied him for a few seconds then leaned forward, resting her forearms on her desk. "I want Marlow to have a good time, but let me tell you something. Don't take it any further than a little fling. She doesn't need to have her heart broken again."

Although he never had serious relationships, and he was definitely nowhere close to settling down, he was irritated with her assumptions. His spine stiffened, and he drew in a deep breath to argue but she didn't give him time.

"I know your type. You're good for a laugh and some great sex, but that's it. Don't go trying to get her to fall in love with you. You and I both know you're not the type to stick around and settle down. Hell, you're the male counterpart of me; so I know where you're coming from, buddy. You leave her heart out of it. If you don't, I'll hunt you down and carve your heart out with a spoon." The determination he saw shimmering in those chocolate brown eyes left little doubt she would do just that.

The door to Marlow's office opened and Ken Moore came out. Liam stood, his feet spread apart and arms crossed over his chest. He was ready to do battle, if need be.

When Liam had met him several hours earlier, he'd genuinely liked the man. Moore struck him as a straight shooter. He was a little too proper and stiff for the two of them to become really good friends, but he struck Liam as someone who really cared about what happened to the company. Saving jobs, he'd told Liam, was the most important thing.

Now, of course, Liam really hated Moore. Nothing the man did changed, but he had a date on Friday with Marlow and he was competition. And, because he was competition, he had to be eliminated from Marlow's sexual landscape. Although Liam had never been territorial before, he had staked his claim on that luscious little body three months ago, and no one else had a right to it. Not that he wanted anything permanent because permanence meant marriage.

Marriage? Even thinking about it stopped his heart. Half of his married friends were divorced and the other half unhappily married. He didn't need those kinds of problems interfering with Campbell and Associates.

Marlow followed Ken out into the outer office, knowing Liam was waiting to confront her. She'd made it through the conference with Ken, hoping she didn't make a fool of herself. Her famous concentration was shot because all she could think about were a pair of green eyes and two of the most talented hands she'd ever felt.

Each time Ken would begin to drone on about something, her mind would wander to that night. She didn't delve into specific memories; if she had, she never would have made it through the meeting. What she did remember was his clean, masculine scent and the way he shuddered when she ran her hand down his chest to his abdomen. His groans and his laughter, and the way he looked at her, his eyes darkened with desire, sent warmth coursing through her blood.

Liam stood by Joey's desk, his arms crossed over his chest, his feet spread apart, looking at Ken as if he were ready to tear his face from his skull. Ken, totally oblivious to most things that didn't plug into the wall, was explaining some of the changes in the October ads to Joey.

Marlow moved and Liam's gaze transferred to her. The dark look of anger shifted, deepening to a look she recognized only too well. Each time he'd looked at her that way, they'd ended up tangled amidst sheets or in the shower. The memory of the shower they took together, the water pouring over them as they sat in the tub as she rode Liam, caused a slow roll of warmth to invade her body. All the moisture in her mouth evaporated because she was sure from the look in his eyes, he was remembering the same thing.

"Well," Ken said, for at least the tenth time, breaking her thoughts away from Liam, "I think these should do." He turned to leave and noticed Liam for the first time. "Ah, Campbell, just the man I wanted to see. Marlow and I just went over the promotions for October, and I was wondering if she could get with you and run the November promotions by you, too."

Marlow stared at Ken, completely surprised by the request. He'd never mentioned anything to her about working with Liam, but she was sure Liam would jump at the chance, just to punish her.

"Of course, Moore. Though, I'm just supposed to observe and then send in a report, this looks like something requiring my *personal* attention."

"Great," he said, giving him his thousand watt smile. "Marlow, I need to talk to you for just a sec. Something I forgot earlier."

"Sure thing, Ken." She followed him out into the hallway.

As soon as the door clicked shut, Joey started to laugh. Not a regular laugh, but a huge knock-you-on-your-ass belly laugh.

"What's so funny, Ms. Vernon?" Liam asked, facing her. Even though she finally stopped laughing, she still had a big, fat smile on her face.

"You," she said with a snort. "Here you were, ready to have a pissing contest to battle Moore, and he didn't even see it." She snorted again.

He gave her what he hoped was his best dirty look, and then turned to look at the door. If he shifted just right, he would be able to see through the tiny rectangular window. He wanted to make sure Moore wasn't touching Marlow.

"You really are pathetic."

He turned to study the woman who "hired" him in the first place. She had spent more time laughing at him than any other woman he knew.

"What do you mean?" he asked, pretending not to know what she was talking about.

"Oh, just you don't need to worry about Ken. He's not for her, so stop worrying."

"I'm not worried about him," he said, completely rendering his words obsolete as soon as he turned to see if he could observe them through the little window. "I thought her father wanted her to get married again. Isn't the appliance the top candidate?"

"I see you've been spending time with Mr. Chambers," she said dryly. "Yes, he is the hand-picked stud." She laughed again when he winced at her wording. "But, although she may date him, and maybe even sleep with him, she won't marry him. They're too much alike. I mean, the way they are, their children would need super intensive therapy to get over all the compulsions they would inherit."

He didn't hear Joey's comment at the end or the door opening behind him, all he heard was the fact Marlow might sleep with Moore. His fists clenched in anger and a red haze of rage blurred his vision.

"The hell she is! He lays one finger on Marlow's little body, and I'll kick his ass to Mexico."

"Liam! What, may I ask, are you thinking?"

He turned to find a horrified Marlow gaping at him, her hand still holding the door open with a cluster of people standing in the hall behind her. All of them looked highly interested in his comments about the boss's daughter.

She shut the door behind her, and he knew she was aware of the curious stares. One little old lady even pressed her face against the window to get a better view.

"Mr. Campbell," she said, anger vibrating from each word, "could I see you in my office?"

"Sure thing," Liam said, casually putting his hands in his pockets and happily sauntering after her.

She was such a cute little thing when she was riled. Rage flowed off her like lava, and those blue eyes snapped with icy anger. Little Miss Marlow sure was a bundle of contradictions.

She held the door open for him, and she shut it with little more than a click. No slamming door for Marlow Jane Smith. He sat in one of the two chairs situated in front of her desk as she walked around and sat down. Her body vibrated with passionate anger, and it was just enough to jump-start his libido.

Okay. So the truth was, it didn't take much to jump-start

his libido around Marlow. This buttoned-down, picture straightening, conservative woman punched his buttons. Maybe it was because he knew about the contradictions. He knew she loved to have her feet rubbed and how she looked when her hair was a tumble of inky waves cascading down her back, her bare shoulders peeking through.

He knew how she moaned his name when she came.

"Mr. Campbell, I really would appreciate it if you wouldn't discuss anything of a personal nature at the office."

She sat with her delicate hands clasped in front of her on the desk, her posture perfect. Most people would think she was the picture of serenity. He knew better. She was clasping her hands so tightly he was amazed there was blood flowing through them. And although she'd banked some of the anger, those blue eyes still held a shimmer of the fury.

"First off, I want you to call me Liam." He stared into her eyes with such steely determination she relinquished that one point with a nod. "Next, I want you to know there is no way in hell I'm going to forget about what went on between us."

She could see there was no way to fight that argument, so she decided to use pity.

"Liam, you have to understand. I can't have the staff gossiping about me. I am sometimes in an uncomfortable position being the boss' daughter." His mouth softened from the hard frown and his eyes showed understanding. "And, although I know I work twice as hard as anyone else, I have to keep my private affairs out of the office."

Just as quickly as the warmth and understanding had crept into his eyes, they vanished.

"Why the hell are you going out with Moore then?"

"I didn't say I couldn't date, I just said discussions about my body," she said, angry about the blush that worked its way up her face, "are out of line. I will lose all respect, and you know it."

His lips turned down in a mulish frown but he said, "Okay."

"I know this may be very normal to have liaisons like we did, but I'm not used to this, as you well know."

"Oh, really," he said, his voice deceptively calm. "You know, no one has ever paid me for sex before you."

"I didn't pay you for sex," she hissed. She took several deep breaths to calm the anger that had boiled up. "First of all, it was Joey who paid."

"What about the hundred dollar tip?"

"That's not what I'm talking about. I'm talking about initially. Second of all, you weren't the one I was supposed to sleep with. I was supposed to sleep with some expert."

"Expert?"

"Yes, Mr. Jones, the *real* Mr. Jones, was supposed to be an expert in, you know." Another wave of heat flowed through her body but it had nothing to do with anger. She glanced down at her desk and noticed her calendar was slightly askew from where she kept it, so she busied herself straightening it.

"Oh?" His voice had deepened, still smooth as whiskey, but with just a touch of roughness. She looked up to see him watching her lust had replaced the sparks of anger.

Slowly, he rose from the chair, not breaking eye contact until he walked behind her. Marlow noticed a ring left by someone's drink, and she tried using a Kleenex to clean it off. He leaned forward, placing his hands on the arms of her chair. She squeezed her eyes shut when she felt his breath on the tender skin behind her ear.

"You forget, Marlow. I know what you look like when you come. I know how you moan, how wet you get," he said, his voice thick with passion.

He bit the skin he had been kissing, and then licked it. The heat spread to other parts of her body, her panties dampened with anticipation.

"Marlow," he said, his voice shaking, "I know how you feel when you come. I know how you tighten around my cock, pulling me, draining me—"

Chapter 6

"You know," Liam whispered in Marlow's ear, "as many times as you came that night, I can't believe you have a problem saying the word, Marlow." Her body throbbed and her pulse doubled. "I thought I had cured you of your *problem*. I thought I was considered an *expert*."

He took her earlobe between his teeth and bit down ever so slightly. Heat pooled in her belly, and her nipples hardened with the first contact. He released her earlobe, and she bit back a moan of protest. His hot lips touched the tender skin just below her lobe.

*   *   *   *

Liam cursed when the phone rang. He had been so close to getting Marlow on her desk. He wanted to reawaken saucy little Jane, and show Marlow there was nothing wrong with her. His blood pulsed with the need to prove to her just how passionate she really was.

When she started talking about the gigolo who was supposed to be the *expert*, he lost control.

Somewhere in the back of his mind, he guessed he knew he was going to seduce her again. It was inevitable. Neither one of them could fight the passion they felt for the other. He would be in Abilene for at least three or four weeks. *A month to work her out of my system, to get back on track.*

"Daddy," she said into the phone and Liam relinquished the arms of her chair and turned to stare out the window. Her cool voice, with just a bit of husky passion in it, washed over him, once again reminding him of her contradictions. That cool voice, those button down clothes, you would think she was some kind of a frigid bitch. But once you unwrapped the package, you found a woman who was as hot as a habanera pepper. Underneath that pale, ivory skin lurked a sensualist. The night they had spent together had proven that. She had to have slept with some real buffoons to go so long without having an orgasm. All he had to do was touch her, and she melted into a puddle of lust.

She hung up the phone, and he glanced down and noticed the bulge in his pants wasn't so obvious, but he figured he'd let her stand before turning around. One of the things he didn't want was for her to be mouth level with his fly. He might come, just from the image.

Her chair squeaked as she stood. Her arm brushed against him as she leaned against the credenza in front of the window. He looked at her from the corner of his eye and wasn't surprised to find her face pink.

She cleared her throat nervously. "Liam, I really don't think it's a good idea for us to do anything intimate again."

Lust drained and anger replaced it. "Honey, let's get this straight. You want me and I want you. There's no way you're going to want to stay away from my bed." She inched away from him, and he realized the anger in his voice, along with his threat, might have frightened her.

"There's no reason for you to lose your temper." Her big blue eyes widened with apprehension. Jesus, he barely raised his voice. *What kind of relationships did this woman have? Did no one ever raise his or her voice?*

"I'm not losing my temper. You'll know when I'm angry." He took a step toward her, and she backed away, the apprehension in her eyes turning into genuine fright. He reigned in his temper, composing himself. "Baby, don't worry, I'd never hurt you."

But she continued to back away until she was on the other side of the desk.

"Liam, I really don't go in for passionate displays of anger."

"Sometimes it's good to let off a little steam," he said, studying her.

"I don't see how that could be, Liam. Someone always gets hurt when the wrong thing is said. Sometimes, those things hurt more than real injuries." He saw a painful memory flash in her eyes. "They last a lot longer."

Jesus, what the hell kind of affairs had this woman had? He thought back to what little she had told him about herself. She'd married young, and now it seemed she only dated men her father handpicked. Not one of them probably ever knew she was a beautiful, passionate woman, full of contradictions and idiosyncrasies. He wouldn't allow her to pull away from him because of them.

He slowly walked around the desk, wondering how something that started out playfully had turned into something so serious.

Contradictions.

"Why don't you let me take you to dinner?" He sidled up beside her.

A small Mona Lisa smile played about her lips, confusing him. "No, I'm taking you." His hope soared, thinking about going home with her and then plummeted to the ground just as fast with her next comment. "My father wants you to eat over at their house tonight. I've been summoned to bring you."

Okay, not the one-on-one orgy fest he'd envisioned, but she still had to take him back to his hotel. And, with a mental shrug, he reminded himself that any time spent with her, would help him attain his goal.

Marlow, naked and willing.

* * * *

Marlow drove Liam to her parents' house in Wylie, a very small suburb outside of Abilene. She glanced over at him. He looked gorgeous, as usual. His chambray shirt appeared soft from many washings, his jeans rode low on his hips, clinging in all the right places. As soon as she parked the car, he jumped out and strode to her side to assist her. The truth of the matter was, he kept touching her, and it disturbed her. Each little touch sent a wave of electricity shooting through her system, warming her blood, and breaking her concentration.

When she had picked him up at his hotel room, she had expected him to try to entice her into his room. But all he did was grab his key card. *Not one word about getting me in the room, or in his bed.* She sighed with disappointment.

Then he had gently taken her elbow and walked down the hall to the elevators. She had changed from her business suit into a soft purple cotton dress. The heat from his hand seeped through the sleeve of her dress. As he held it, he moved his fingers ever so softly. A delicious furl of heat radiated from her elbow and gave her a soft, glowing feeling before she could stop it.

This time, he walked on the opposite side as before, taking her elbow and giving it the same treatment. She shivered in reaction to the touch and not the cool evening breeze. His lips twitched. He knew just what he was doing. The problem was she wasn't sure she wanted him to stop. Even though she knew she shouldn't, she longed for Liam to slide his hand up her arm and brush the side of her breast. Her blood warmed at the thought of his fingers brushing her tender skin.

When they reached the front door, she breathed a sigh of relief and removed her elbow from Liam's hand, since the doorway was too small for the two of them to fit through side-by-side.

The aroma of potatoes roasting in the oven filled the air, and she knew her father had started the grill outside for the steaks. Liam shut the door with a click, and followed her down the hall.

"Your folks live here long?" he asked.

"No, they moved in a few years ago when I moved out. Mummy didn't want to clean that big of a house."

"I would think they'd have a maid."

She laughed and turned to face him. He stood with the hall light overhead, highlighting the golden strands in his hair and adding darkness to those green eyes, a bemused expression on his face.

"What?" she asked. He kept staring at her…at her lips, unnerving her.

"You just don't laugh that way that often." His lips curved into a gentle smile. She must have shown her distress because the next thing he said was, "Now don't go pokering all up on me. I just gave you a compliment." He crossed his arms over his chest. "Now, you tell me why it's funny that your mother doesn't have a maid."

"We had a few when I was younger. Mummy drove them

all away. You'll understand as soon as you meet her."

"Meet who?" her mother said behind her.

She turned to find her mother, every bit the English lady, standing in the doorway that led to the kitchen. Her blonde hair was styled into a fashionable chignon, her makeup was perfectly applied.

"Mummy, I would like you to meet Liam Campbell. Liam, this is mummy, or as she likes to be called by very attractive young men, Clarice."

Her mother's regal pose dissolved, and she smiled the same familiar smile that had greeted Marlow when she came in second at the spelling bee. "Oh, pooh. Marly just likes to poke fun at me." She walked forward and gave Marlow a hug and a peck on the cheek. Her mother looped her arm around Marlow's waist and pulled her to her side, as if to defend her.

"Well, now I know why all the ladies were in such a twitter when I stopped by the office today. How do you do, Liam?"

"I do just fine, Clarice." His lady-killer smile was back, and she could practically feel her mother melting. *Was no woman safe from the man?*

"Now I have potatoes in the oven, and the salad is almost finished. Your father is trying to insist we eat outside, but I told him that was ridiculous. You know he never listens to me. Every now and then, he listens and we advert disaster, but he usually doesn't pay attention to a thing I say. You remember, Marly, when we were on that trip to Canada, and your father wouldn't allow me to read a map? We never would have found our way out of that snowstorm if we hadn't found that diner. Oh, and there was that time your father decided to use extra lighter fluid on the grill. It cost a fortune to repair the porch roof."

As usual, this was all said without taking a breath. Mummy had walked down the hall, straightening pictures while she talked and was now dusting off a table that didn't need to be dusted. Marlow glanced over to see Liam's reaction. He watched her mother with a little smile and then turned to look at her and she saw laughter in his eyes.

"Quit flirting with my women," her father boomed from behind them. She looked over her shoulder to find her father with his usual jovial I-had-two-beers smile spread across his face.

"Hey, daddy," she said returning his smile. No matter how mad she got at her father, she could never stay mad at the man who loved her and her mother so much. Even though she wasn't the boy he wanted, she knew he loved her all the same.

"Don't 'hey daddy' me, young lady. Get that man a beer and bring him out here."

She went to do her father's bidding. Liam followed behind her, making some inane comment to her mother about the house, and she almost laughed. Here was a man who she paid to have sex with her, someone who, if he could be believed, planned on seducing her, and he walked through her parents' house commenting on the Italian ceramic tile in the kitchen. Her life was getting a little too strange for words.

* * * *

Liam sat across the table from Marlow, her mother on his right and her father on his left, and watched the interaction between daughter and parents. From what she'd said, he had assumed she had some kind of a strained, proper relationship with them. From what he observed, the situation was nothing close to his assumptions.

Marlow was the same height and petite stature as her

mother, but Marlow's hair was a sleek mass of ink, while
Clarice's hair resembled spun gold. They shared the same blue
eyes and even the same gorgeous skin, but both were more pronounced on Marlow because of her black hair. That was the
only thing she must have gotten from her father.

Well over six feet, Ham had salt and pepper hair Liam was
sure had been as dark as Marlow's at one time. He had a boisterous laugh and an easy personality.

He studied Marlow further, her full, rosy lips curved into a
smile that brightened her whole being. When she let her guard
down, she was such a warm person.

That one thought brought back all the memories of that
night. The feel of her skin against his, the way she moaned
when he touched her, that husky laugh that drove him insane.

He cursed himself silently when he realized he was sitting
in between her parents with a full-fledged boner. How the hell
did he get himself into this position in the first place? Oh, yeah,
some little woman approached him in a bar and said she paid
him for sex.

"Now, Liam, I want to know what you think about the
store you saw today," Ham said.

Liam gathered his wits and realized, after he found out
who little Ms. Jane Smith actually was, he hadn't paid attention
to one thing about the store. Other than the way everyone
seemed very friendly with Marlow.

"We didn't spend much time at the store, Daddy. We had
to get back because of my conference with Ken," she said, her
voice controlled and cool. All the warmth in her voice had
faded.

"Well, what was so important about that?" he father grumbled.

Her face turned pinker and for the second time that day, jealousy stabbed him. Just what the hell went on behind that door when she had her "conference" with Moore? He knew what he would do with Marlow if he had her behind closed doors; he'd have her up on the desk so fast, she wouldn't know what hit her. Hell, he had been moving that way when her father called.

"We had to discuss some of the upcoming promotions. And we're having problems with that same vendor."

As Marlow and her father started discussing the vendor, he thought back to the night they'd spent together. She'd been so skittish at first, like this afternoon when he lost his temper. The only time she seemed to relax was when she had been in control. Well, he could understand that.

Liam was known for being a man with strong appetites. He loved women, and he loved making love. But, he always made sure he controlled the situation. Liam had learned at a young age that a man who had no control over his life, all aspects of it, was a weak man. He was a passionate lover. Women were to be appreciated for their intelligence as well as their bodies, and he always made sure they enjoyed themselves. But he remained in control, calling the shots and ending the relationship if it got out of hand.

He glanced at Marlow as she coolly suggested what they should do about the situation with the vendor to her father. One of the most amazing things he had ever seen, in or out of the bedroom, was that cool, composed woman fall apart. But thinking back, he realized she hadn't once relaxed when it appeared he ran the show. In fact, the first time on the couch, she had held his hands back, controlling the rhythm of their lovemaking.

Then it came to him. She was a woman who had never had any control over her life. She had married the man her parents had chosen, dated men her father picked out, hell, her father probably bought the car out in the driveway. Her reserved demeanor hid a passionate streak that sparkled if she were left in control.

"What do you think, Liam?" Ham asked.

Surprised, he glanced at Ham, realizing he wanted his input on the situation they had been discussing. He decided to put his plan into action.

"Well, I think Marlow knows what she's talking about. You should follow her advice."

He looked at Marlow with an admiration that had nothing to do with her intelligence. Suspicion darkened her violet eyes.

"Hmmm, I'll think about it. Well, why don't you join me in a game of pool?"

"I'd like to take a rain check on that, Ham. I want to get an early start tomorrow and that drive from Dallas was long."

"Will do. Marlow, you take this boy back to the hotel and treat him right."

Surprise lit her eyes but she banked it. Liam could think of about a thousand things she could do to treat him right, but he knew Ham didn't have that in mind.

"Sure thing, Daddy," she said, the irritation dripping from her voice. He didn't know if that was for him or Ham, but he didn't care. He had the means to get little Ms. Marlow back into his bed and show her just how good they could be together.

He almost rubbed his hands together, thinking about what was in store for them.

Chapter 7

"Aren't you coming up to say goodnight?" Liam asked Marlow a little over thirty minutes later. It had taken at least ten minutes to extricate themselves from her parents' house, with Liam promising he would be over to watch the Cowboy game the Sunday after next.

She'd driven him straight back to his hotel, thankful her apartment wasn't on the way. Marlow looked at him, which was hard in the dark car. A light on the side of the hotel shone harshly on them, hardening his usually pleasant face. With the looks he sent her during dinner, she knew exactly what he had been thinking. She knew, because it took every bit of her will power not to think about the same thing. The only problem was, every now and then she would relax, and without any effort, her mind would drift back to the things he said to her in her office. She wasn't sure if she had to drive by her apartment complex, she wouldn't take him home with her.

"No, Liam. I have an early morning coming up," she said, appalled her voice was huskier than usual. His face split into a wolfish grin, and even in the dark car, she could see his green eyes twinkle. She knew he had noted the husky tenor of her voice.

"Well." He took her hand in his. "I guess since you are the boss, I'll let you call the shots."

Liam looked like the proverbial cat that ate the canary. He was up to something she just didn't know what it was. With his other hand, he released his seatbelt and leaned over to kiss her.

Excitement tingled down her spine. Oh, she wanted that kiss. She wanted his hot, wet lips on hers, kissing her senseless, so she would forget about responsibilities, forget she had a very boring date planned for Friday night.

He was about a centimeter away from kissing her, when that thought made her jerk away from him. Jeez, what the hell was wrong with her? Here she was, a few days before her date with Ken and she was about to play kissy face with Liam. With the darkness of the night surrounding her, comforting her, she forgot why it was wrong to start up with Liam. A man who could have any woman in town and wanted her for only one reason: revenge.

"Listen." She braced one hand on his chest.

He shifted slightly and she could feel the hard muscle moving beneath her hand. Liam was a man in top shape, muscular and lean, and he was so hot. His body radiated so much heat. Marlow remembered curling up next to him in bed, seeking his warmth. She could feel his heart beat speed up beneath her hand and surprised, she looked up.

"See what you do to me, baby?" he asked, his voice deep and not very steady. "Just one little touch and you have my heart leaping out of my chest."

"Liam." Her voice a desperate plea. She tried to pull her hand away, but she wasn't quick enough. He placed his hand on top of hers, trapping it against his chest.

"I don't think you know your own power," he said, his voice deepening just a bit. "You are, by far, one of the most seductive women I know." She let go a disbelieving snort. "Really. On the outside, you're cool and contained," he said, caressing her hand. "But underneath that cool exterior, beneath all the proper manners and picture straightening, lurks one hot, passionate woman. She's wanting to be the one in control, but you keep pulling back."

"Liam." This time, she almost whimpered. Heat from his words was spreading through her body. The darkness of the car, his whispered seduction, the glowing warmth slithering through her system, were making it hard for her to remember why she wanted to go home in the first place. She leaned toward him but lights from another car illuminated the interior of hers, and she viewed the totally satisfied smile on Liam's face. Jerking away, she surprised him and easily freed her hand.

"Marlow," he growled.

"No, you won't seduce me with the honeyed words you use all the time. I'm not as easy as your usual women and I'll thank you to remember it." She saw a spark of something that might have been hurt in his eyes, but she ignored it. Distancing herself was the only way to save herself pain.

He studied her for a second or two, let out a weary sigh. "I'll let you go tonight, Marlow, because you're the one in charge. But that doesn't mean I'm going to let you go forever." He leaned over, kissed her cheek, then whispered in her ear, "Sweet dreams, Marlow." She shivered as his breath heated her ear, sending hot sparks bolting through her.

He pulled back from her, his eyes hot with desire, hesitated for just a second, then got out of the car. As if in a trance, she watched him walk up to the side door of the hotel, use his key card in the security lock and slip inside. She sighed; knowing half of the sigh was relief and the other half was disappointment. Unfortunately, the disappointment was sharper than the relief.

* * * *

By eight o'clock the next morning, Marlow had been at work for over an hour, trying to work through the problems that had arisen with their December promotions. Every now and then, Liam would pop into her thoughts, but she'd been stalwart and pushed him to the recesses of her mind. She heaved a sigh, knowing no matter how many times she pushed him back, he would pop back up, breaking her concentration.

She looked down at the proposal she'd given her father and sighed again. Her father had given her the job in charge of promotions a year ago. Many people, people who didn't know her very well, thought she got the job because she was the boss's daughter. The truth of the matter was she got the job, in spite of being the boss's daughter.

Her parents had been convinced she would marry, so they had never thought she would go to UT and get her MBA, expecting to work in the family business. She had worked in the grocery stores as a teenager and did a little work at a couple of stores in Austin, learning the business from the ground up, just like her father. Unfortunately, it had been six years since she returned, and her father still didn't take any of her suggestions seriously.

Oh, if Ken, who had less store experience than she did, agreed with her, which he normally did, then her father would go with the idea. But, Ken and her father both disagreed with the promotion of the contest she had suggested to beat out the competition.

Unlike other retail businesses, grocery business peaked before Thanksgiving. They generally had a steady business up until Christmas, but the last few years, Smith's sales had declined a little each year.

Consumers wanted convenience. Smith's was sorely lacking in that area. Where a lot of other grocery chains had remodeled existing stores to meet the demands of the busy Texas family, only Smith's newer ones had upgraded to ready-made meals, coffee bars, and banking facilities within them. Her father had nixed her idea to begin a total rehab of the older stores. He ignored her warnings of the market research and built more stores, all from capital, never credit, and planned to add ten more, bringing the total to seventy-five, by the time he retired in five years. A store for each year of his life. The only problem was, while the newer stores in areas like Dallas and Houston were doing great, those in the smaller cities and towns were just keeping their heads above water, some of them dipping under every now and then. Those small town stores made up about seventy-five percent of their revenue, and no matter how well the ones in the big cities did, they would all go under if they didn't do something quickly.

So, to entice the customers into their smaller stores, Marlow had suggested giving away a two hundred dollar shopping spree the twelve days before Christmas. They wouldn't include their bigger stores, whose revenue remained steady this time of year, just the fifty smaller ones. Marlow knew this, coupled with some smaller promotions involving donations to the needy, would really help the stores in question. She wasn't letting the idea go, she was going to fight this one to the death.

"Well, I would hate to be the one who caused that scowl," Joey said from the doorway.

Joey was, once again, in fine form today. The red dress she wore stopped just short of being indecent, her blonde hair was styled bigger than usual, and her makeup was perfect. If she didn't love Joey so much, Marlow would surely hate her.

"Oh," she said with a sigh filled with disgust, "just trying to work out a way to convince my father to go with my twelve days of Christmas shopping spree."

Joey rolled her eyes and walked forward. She placed a cup of coffee, doctored just the way Marlow loved it, on her desk.

"Go ahead, you need it this morning." She must have given her a suspicious look because Joey explained, "You look tired. I figured someone kept you up last night, or, judging by the unsatisfied look on your face, thinking about someone was keeping you up last night. How did dinner go?"

Marlow took a sip and allowed the warmth of the coffee to seep through her. "Oh, my mother loves him, my father wants him as a son, and I'm stuck looking like the sore thumb."

"Hmmm. Nothing else happened?" She seated herself in one of the chairs in front of the desk.

"No, not really. He just flirted, that's all." Joey gave her an unbelieving look. "Okay, he tried to get me up to his room last night."

"I figured something like that." Her lips curved into a little satisfied smile. "So, after he tried something yesterday afternoon in here——"

"How did you know about that?"

"I am all knowing," she said in an overly theatrical voice.

"Besides, you blush like crazy. And you were flushed and nervous when you finally came out. Knowing the kind of man Liam is, well, I figured he would try again."

"His seduction has more to do with revenge than anything else."

Joey gave her another disbelieving look. "Revenge for what?"

"Revenge because I didn't beg him to be my sex slave."

"That's something that would have made my dreams come true," Liam said from the doorway. He was wearing another dark gray suit, green shirt, and another outrageous tie. Something with palm trees against a black background. Standing there, the sunlight glinting off the golden highlights in his hair, humor lightening his eyes, and a smile softening his features, he looked good enough to eat. That sight brought about all kind of delicious thoughts, and her face heated.

Joey looked from her red face to Liam's and said, "I'm too young for the thoughts flying around this office. I'm out of here."

"Oh, Joey, let me know when Ken gets in."

"Sure thing, boss woman," Joey said, shutting the door behind her and leaving her to face her nemesis and her fantasy come to life.

Liam raised an eyebrow and asked, "Boss woman?"

"It's just a joke—an old one at that. What can I do for you this morning?" she asked and then immediately regretted the question because his smile became a grin and the light in his eyes deepened into something she knew was not humor.

* * * *

Liam stared at her for a second, trying to decide if he should go into graphic detail on what she could do for him this morning. He was positive if he did, she would go running for cover, and he would never get any closer to his goal.

"Well, I was going to take a tour of another store today, but Ken already agreed to do that with me."

At first, the relief he saw in her eyes irritated him. Then he realized, maybe she wasn't so cool to his ideas after all. Maybe she was contemplating jumping his bones. *Good*. He was tired and edgy from too little sleep and too many thoughts of her. He had gone to bed last night, but one little kiss, just a touch of his lips to her cheek, kept him horny for hours. It didn't help he had taken a shower before going to dinner and he could still smell her lavender scent on his hands.

Around two that morning, he gave up and took a cold shower, washing away the scent and a little of the lust. But, not four hours later, he woke up, sweat pouring off of him and a tent in the sheets a whole troop of cub scouts could use.

He really didn't get it. The woman was not overtly sexy, the way he usually liked his women. She just wasn't comfortable with her sexuality. When he hit upon the idea of giving her control, he really thought he had struck gold. But Liam was not a man used to allowing the woman the first move. They may work to get his attention, but he never relinquished control of the length or the intensity of the relationship.

Marlow was different. She needed control because she didn't have any in her life. Oh, she didn't live at home with her parents, but hell, she worked for her father, who ignored every suggestion she had. He handpicked her husband and planned on handpicking her second, if Ken was any indication. On top of all of that, she apparently had been to bed with some real idiots. The woman burned hotter than a firecracker when she got going, the man just needed to light the fuse.

"How did you sleep last night, Ms. Marlow?" he asked.

Her eyes narrowed and she didn't say anything for a few seconds and he was sure she was probably weighing whether or not he was being facetious.

"I slept fine," she replied, her voice as cold as a blue northern.

"Hmm, in awfully early for someone who slept fine."

She went back to studying the paper in front of her. Then once the silence had stretched and Liam was feeling a little uncomfortable, she looked up and said, "I come in about six-thirty every day, Liam. I like to come in when it's quiet and I can get a lot of work done, without any interruptions."

She pushed her glasses back up her nose and went back to studying the sheet in front of her. When he glanced down, he noticed the paper she was actually "reading" was upside down. *Well, well, little Ms. Marlow was not as immune to me as she would like me to believe.*

"Just in case you wondering, I didn't sleep well at all. *I couldn't stop thinking about you.*" He paused and saw her swallow and the pulse fluttering in her slender neck. Oh, he wished he could lean across the desk and kiss that spot. "So, there I was, taking a cold shower at two in the morning and it didn't do any good."

The paper trembled slightly in her hand and she licked her lips. He almost groaned out loud when he saw her tongue dart out to lick her plump lower lip. She worried her lower lip with her teeth and licked it again. The heat that had settled in his stomach took a quick slide to his groin.

Slowly, he walked around the desk, but she still didn't look up. Instead, she had abandoned the paper and moved onto straightening her desk. She spent an inordinate amount of time placing her desk calendar and her penholder in exactly the right spot.

He leaned against the desk, crossing his legs at his ankles and gently lifted her chin with his finger. She swallowed nervously.

"Stood in that cold shower for twenty minutes. But then, I guess it reminded me of our shower together. You remember that, don't you?" Her eyes turned so violet, they resembled smoke. He knew then she remembered the same thing he did. Him sitting in the tub with the shower running, her on top of him, riding him hard as the water streamed down on top of them.

He swallowed nervously. *Jesus, I planned on seducing her, not losing control myself.* He took a deep breath. His finger still held her chin up; her eyes were smoky with passion. He leaned forward, wanting to take a taste of the lip she was biting and was within an inch of doing so, when there was a sharp knock at the door, and it burst open.

"Look who had to stop by for a second with some papers and wanted to see you," Joey said. A dark-haired man, a little shorter than Joey, stood next to her, her arm linked through his. His dark brown hair was cut in an unmemorable fashion and his suit looked more expensive than Liam's. He was a typical Texan, wearing his cowboy boots with the suit.

Marlow jerked back from him, her eyes widening just a bit when she saw the visitor. She stood and walked around the desk. The man released Joey and embraced her.

"How ya doing, kid?" he asked as he lifted her off of her feet. He set her down, and then released her, after holding onto her a shade too long in Liam's opinion.

"Pretty good now I've joined the thirty-something

crowd." The overly friendly man was looking down at Marlow, affection in his voice and mannerisms.

"So now you're an old maid, maybe you'll reconsider our marriage," he said. She gave a tinkle of a laugh that had Liam doing a double take. He had never heard such a flirty laugh from the woman since he had known her. Then what the man said registered and he realized this was the ex. He glanced at Joey and saw the self-satisfied smile on her face and he knew then she saw the flash of jealousy.

"Your wife might have something to say about that," she said. He shifted from one foot to the other and the ex looked over at him and his eyes narrowed. Marlow realized Liam had captured the man's attention.

"Oh, Ben I would like you to meet Liam Campbell. Liam, this is Ben Alden, the infamous ex-husband." Her voice was filled with laughter and there was no wariness in her manner.

Liam offered his hand, thinking the man would let go of Marlow, but Ben kept his arm firmly around Marlow's waist and reached around with his left hand instead.

"Campbell. I heard you're here to help with the sagging sales."

"Well, that's company business. I'm not sure if I feel comfortable discussing it with you." *Okay, a little rude, but the bastard deserved it.* And if he didn't let go of Marlow soon, he was going to do something about it.

"Hmmm, well being district manager for the west Texas area, I figure you can discuss it with me." His wide, stupid face had a smirk on it that Liam would like to smack off and he was about to step forward, when Joey stopped him.

"Liam, I think Ken was looking for you earlier. He said something about going to a couple stores today."

"Well, Liam, it was nice to meet you. I'm sure we'll have time to discuss the business strategy you have in mind later," Ben said, his voice mocking Liam.

"Sure thing, Ben." Liam turned away from him and concentrated on the little woman whose waist was still encircled with the man's arm. "Marlow, we're scheduled to have lunch to discuss the promotions you have in mind and how they'll work with my strategy. Would eleven-thirty be okay?"

Her eyes widened at the request and probably, because he looked directly into them, without wavering. "Sure, Liam."

"See ya later, Marlow." He looked toward the ex with the overly friendly hands and said, "Alden." And strode to the door. He needed a little time to regroup and concentrate on something other than little Ms. Marlow's body and how it made him feel to have another man touch it.

* * * *

"Now, why don't you tell me why you're being so touchy feely?" Marlow asked dryly.

Ben's eyes widened with mock innocence, and then he laughed. "I never could get anything by you." He squeezed her waist and then let her go. Marlow walked around and sat in her chair. "I had to drop off some papers before I headed out to Sweetwater and I wanted to ask you something really important."

Chapter 8

Ben shifted from foot to foot uncharacteristically nervous. Even through their horrible wedding and disastrous six-month marriage, Ben had been the one who had kept the two of them sane. When their parents had pushed them towards marriage, Marlow, who was nineteen, and Ben, who was a couple of months away from legal drinking age, succumbed to the pressure.

Throughout their childhood, Ben and Marlow's families had spent most holidays together. More and more, they found themselves drawn to each other. They both excelled in math and by her senior year of high school, Ben was finishing up his junior year at Abilene Christian University, majoring in business administration. Other than their interest in business, Ben and Marlow found camaraderie in their personalities. Ben came a boisterous family, two very outgoing parents and a sister who was homecoming queen each year.

Marlow, an only child and quiet natured, found a friend in Ben whose temperament paralleled hers. For two people so alike and with many of the same interests, marriage might have been ideal, if they each had not viewed the other as siblings. Marlow's first experience with sex happened on her wedding night with a man she'd always viewed more like a brother. And Liam wondered where she got her sexual hang-ups.

"Spill it, Ben."

"Janice is pregnant again, and we've finally made it through the third month," he said.

Marlow jumped up with a whoop, ran around the desk, and gave him a huge bear hug, almost knocking him off of his feet. His arms closed around her and just for a moment, the warmth of happiness filled her.

She pulled back from the embrace. "So, how is Mommy doing? Are they going to keep her in bed the whole time?"

His nervousness returned and he released her and walked to the window. "No, she's free until maybe the sixth month. I'm just so worried about her. I would be fine if we hadn't lost the last one in the twelfth week."

Ben and Janice, his wife for over five years, had been trying to have a baby for most of their marriage. Janice had a problem carrying the baby and this made her fourth pregnancy. "I told her this is the last time." He shoved his hands in his pockets. "If something happens to this baby, we're going to adopt," he said, his voice almost breaking. "It's just not worth it."

Marlow walked around the desk, and entwined her hands around his waist and placed her cheek on his back. He placed his hand on top of hers. "Janice and I, well, if this pregnancy goes to term, we want you to be the godmother."

"Oh, Ben, I would love it! Are you sure you don't want anyone else? I'm sure your sister——" She stopped when he let out a bark of laughter that had little to do with amusement.

Unlike her parents, Ben's had disowned him when their

marriage fell apart. His sister, one of Marlow's best friends at the time, followed suit, and refuse to talk to either of them.

"Well, then, I accept." He squeezed her hand. Her door opened and she let go of him and turned around as Ken and a very angry Liam stared at them.

"Ben," Ken said, apparently had no problem finding the woman he was taking to dinner on Friday night hugging her ex-husband. "Good. I thought maybe you might want to help me show Liam around today."

"I'd love to but I'm scheduled to do some interviewing in Sweetwater," Ben said with a huge grin on his face.

"Well, I guess we can go then. Campbell, you ready?"

Liam looked from Marlow to Ben and back to her again, his eyes narrowed in suspicion. "Yes," he said curtly.

He ignored the two men, looking only at her for a few very uncomfortable moments. She nervously licked her bottom lip and he followed the movement with his green gaze. His nostrils flared as he took a deep breath and her nipples tightened almost painfully as a spark of heat flared in her stomach. Ben cleared his throat and Liam's attention switched to him. "I'll see you at lunch, Marlow." He left, Ken trailing behind him.

"Well, been a long time since I've seen a man that determined about a woman," Ben remarked. "You said this is the new consultant?"

"Yes," Marlow said with a sigh. No matter how many times she convinced herself she could and would resist the man, she wasn't really sure she would be able to when they were alone.

"He seems to have taken an interest in you," Ben said casually. She turned to look at him. He studied her with a serious look on his face. "An interest you seem to reciprocate."

"Good Lord, where on earth did you get an idea like that?" she asked, and was mortified to find her voice unsteady.

"Come on, Marlow, I've known you longer than anyone but your parents, and the sparks flying between the two of you could set off a wildfire in a thunderstorm."

She smiled at the analogy and then frowned. "You don't think Ken noticed, do you?"

Ben snorted, then he lost his humor again. "Don't tell me you're dating Ken."

"Okay, I won't tell you."

"Marlow," he said a warning tone in his voice, "you have to quit dating these losers your father hires. They aren't good enough for you."

"Daddy had no intentions after that last mistake with Vic." Only Joey and Ben really knew what had gone on when she broke things off with the loser. "Ken is an interesting man."

Ben looked skeptical. "He's about as interesting as a paper bag."

"Ben! Now you sound like Joey."

He laughed, not at all insulted. "I knew there was something I liked about that girl."

"And, there's nothing going on between Liam and me," she said with little conviction. She returned to her seat behind her desk and he sank into one of the chairs. "Besides, what do you have against Ken? He's intelligent, well-dressed, and *he* remembered my birthday." Hoping against hope she would make him feel guilty.

"Marlow, don't even try that with me. We had just found out Janice was pregnant. What I want to know is, why are you avoiding answering the question?"

She fidgeted with a couple of pens on her desk and swiveled her creaky chair around. Marlow didn't look him in the eye when she repeated, "There's nothing going on."

"So, that's the way you're going to play it," he said, and she looked up. His deep brown eyes showed only concern. "I just want to make sure you're careful. I don't trust him where you're concerned. Hell, I don't trust any man you come in contact with because all you do is work. Your father handpicks most of them, which means they probably have ulterior motives. Just promise me, if you need me, you'll give me a call. Or Janice. Lord knows, you've listened to us enough over the last few years with our baby making problems."

She smiled at him and fought a pang of envy. Marlow never begrudged him his happiness, but every now and then, she wished she'd found someone like he did and could go on with her life. Although she wasn't sure how good she would be, she longed to be a mother.

"I will. And, I'm sure you need to get going. Are you keeping this a secret?" she asked.

"Yeah, if you don't mind not telling anyone. Janice and I thought you should know. You're the only sis I have left."

A lump formed in her throat and it took a lot of effort to swallow over it. It had taken several years to find the easy camaraderie they'd shared as kids, and she thanked the Lord every day they were able to salvage their friendship.

"And remember. Pretty boy does anything to hurt you you let me know. I'll make sure I make him cry like a little girl."

She smiled. "I may just hold you to that, Ben."

* * * *

By ten-thirty that morning, Liam had enough of Smith's grocery stores, enough of Ken Moore and enough of waiting patiently after leaving Marlow in her office with her ex-husband. An ex she seemed comfortable enough cuddling up to. The hot flash of jealousy that had rushed through him when he found her with her arms wrapped around her ex surprised him. He had never been particularly territorial.

The most embarrassing thing was he wanted Alden to know she was taken, at least at the moment. He had resisted walking into her office, grabbing her by her black hair, and pulling her against his body, kissing her long and hard. So, he conveyed it by giving her a look that let her know they had unfinished business. And, from that one little interlude, he knew she was aware of him. Her eyes had darkened to smoky blue, she had licked her full lower lip, and he would bet his left nut her nipples were puckered, although the shapeless suit she wore didn't show a thing.

"And one of the things we tried to get through to her was spending money in the bigger markets is a better risk," Ken said, his monotone voice droning on. "But really, Marlow has some good ideas."

At the sound of her name, he turned to look at Ken, but he had turned down the bread aisle. Liam backtracked and headed in his direction. He stood beside a thin, tall man with black hair, wearing a t-shirt that advertised chewing tobacco and a pair of jeans. He realized this might be the vendor Marlow and her father were discussing. If he hadn't been fantasizing about what he could do to that little body, he might know what this was all about.

"As long as we understand each other on this one, Chet. Ms. Smith was not too happy to find out what you were doing."

The man threw Ken a rude look he never saw because he had started to rearrange the chips. Chet pulled his bread carrier down the aisle and never said another word.

"I'm going to grab one of the kids and have them work on this mess. It looks like we had a run on the chips," Ken said as he stood up. He walked away, leaving Liam a little uncomfortable with the malicious feelings he had toward the man. He had defended Marlow and he seemed like the kind of guy who cared a lot about the stores. Still, Liam knew, there was no way in hell he was going to be nice to Ken until the man understood Marlow was his.

With that mental note, he followed Ken down the aisle and realized it was time to return to the office.

* * * *

Marlow and Liam sat in her office eating lunch. They'd planned on going out to one of the local favorites again, but things had conspired against them and Liam ran out while Marlow worked with her father and Ken. One of their managers from San Angelo had run off, left his wife and resigned with no notice. Not such a big problem, but he ran off with his first assistant manager, or second key, who was fifteen years younger, leaving them with a newly trained assistant, who was the third key, and no other management for the store. With Ben in Sweetwater, it was decided Ken would go down and take care of the problem and hopefully, by tomorrow they would have a game plan.

She let out a weary sigh and Liam said, "Long day already, huh?"

Marlow looked at him, at his boyishly crooked smile that only showed one of his dimples and the sympathetic light in his green eyes. Unlike a lot of the other men she knew, Liam never blinked an eye when she said she had to stick around because of work. He had taken orders for sandwiches and returned. Her father had grumbled and headed back to his own office with his sandwich and Ken said he would eat on the road leaving Liam and Marlow alone.

They had scooted their chairs up to her desk, and, although it would drive her crazy thinking about the crumbs, they ate their lunch in her office.

She closed her eyes, rubbed her temples, and leaned back in her chair. "Yes. But, with retail, things like this always happen. I'm sure you know that. One year, the computers when out the day before Thanksgiving in one of busiest stores. It was a nightmare."

"Hmmm." He sounded much closer than before. She opened her eyes to find him leaning towards her, sniffing.

"Are you smelling me?" she asked, thinking it was the silliest question she had ever asked.

"Yes. You smell good, Marlow. I would say good enough to eat, but I'm sure you'd get irritated with me if I did." He closed his eyes, leaned a little closer. "You smell like a field of lavender, with a dash of musky woman. Hmmm."

"Liam," she said weakly because now she noticed his cologne and how it mixed with his own scent of a mixture of outdoors and musky man and her heartbeat sped up, bouncing against her chest.

"You know, for months now I could not get that lavender scent out of my head. The worst part would be walking down the street and getting a faint, lingering smell of it from someone or something. Automatically, I thought of you and our night together. Instant arousal. When we were introduced, I should've known when I smelled you there was something familiar about you."

He leaned an inch closer, his eyes still closed, and sniffed again. When the urge to lean closer to him almost overwhelmed her, she bolted out of the chair, apparently not startling him. He lazily opened his eyes, leaned back in the chair, and studied her as she walked around the desk. His heavy-lidded green gaze never left her face, he reminded her of a leopard stalking his prey. That image brought back his words "good enough to eat" and heat crept up her neck and finally into her face.

"There I would be, minding my own business, and that scent would invade my senses and seep into my soul."

His voice had grown rough with his arousal, causing heat to curl into her belly, licking at her senses, heightening her awareness. He stood, and she couldn't help looking down his long length.

Even under his dress shirt, she could see the lean muscles in his arms as they bunched when he moved. She remembered his chest; how she loved sliding her hand along the muscled pecs, lingering on his copper nipples because she knew it drove him crazy. His abs were lean but not overly sculpted, and she remembered placing kisses as she moved down, watching it quiver in reaction. She got to the waistband of his pants and her eyes dipped lower to the tented material and his obvious arousal.

Her face burned brighter and she quickly glanced up to see him with a painful smile on his face.

"You see. You don't even have to touch me." He walked around the desk. Powerless to move, she watched him walk closer, passion darkening his eyes. "You have no idea how much control you have over me. I'm powerless to resist you, but you seem to have no problem whatsoever." He walked behind her, and stood so close, his breath tickled the fine hairs at the nape of her neck. He didn't touch her, but whispered in her ear, "You know, if we wouldn't have been interrupted yesterday, we would have ended up on this desk then."

She closed her eyes and swallowed convulsively. "It was painful to stop, wasn't it, Marlow?" he asked, drawing out her name. "I ached for you last night. Did you ache, Marlow? Did you think about my hands?" He lightly skimmed his hand down her arm. "I thought about touching you. I thought about how soft your skin is. How it felt to have your soft skin under my fingers."

He pushed her chair out of the way, and turned her around, backing her up until her rear end hit the edge of the desk. Gently, he cupped her face with each one of his hands, gently rubbing her cheeks with his thumbs. He leaned forward and, for the life of her, she couldn't stop. She wanted that kiss to ease the ache, to make her feel whole.

She leaned up and he bent down to capture her lips. This was no tender kiss, no nibbling. He took full possession. His tongue swept into her mouth, tangling with hers. She could taste his passion and the coffee he had with lunch. His hands slid around to the small of her back as he moved to fit her body into his.

Liam's muscular chest pressed against her breasts and she almost cried with relief as her hardened nipples pressed against him. She wound her arms around his neck, her fingers sliding over his corded muscles.

His mouth left hers and her head fell back as he placed wet kisses down her neck. About every other kiss, his tongue flicked out, leaving a path of hot, wet skin behind.

He opened the first two buttons of her blouse, and his head dipped down. His tongue slid between her breasts, sending a delicious shiver through her. Marlow knew, on principle, she should stop this. It was the middle of the afternoon, in her office, where anyone could walk in at any moment.

"Liam," she gasped, and he hesitated just a moment, placing another open-mouthed kiss on the swell of each breast before he raised his head. When she saw his eyes, dilated with passion and brimming with lust, she hesitated, and then said, "Anyone could walk in on us."

"No, I locked the door." His deep voice simmered with barely controlled passion. He dipped his head again, and the rest of her buttons gave way and cool air chilled her skin when he pulled her blouse off her shoulders. "Your skin is so sweet, Marlow. I didn't have enough time to taste every inch of it that night." He expertly unhooked the front closure of her bra and her breasts sprang free. Without looking away from her, he positioned her arms behind her on the desk, causing her back to arch slightly.

Liam bent down and licked one of her hardened nipples and Marlow decided she didn't care if it was the middle of the day and they were in her office. He flicked it with his tongue, once, then twice and finally drew the whole nipple into his mouth, sucking and rolling his tongue around it. Each time his tongue went around her nipple, heat radiated out from there and coursed throughout her body.

Liam stopped and drew away and she moaned in protest. She looked down to find him looking up at her. Her pink nipple was glistening and puckered. He didn't say a word, just bent his head, and continued his assault on the other. While he laved her nipple, his hands encircled her waist and he picked her up, placing her on her desk. He immediately moved into the vee of her legs, and his arousal, hard and hot, pressed against her. His hands crept down to the edge of her skirt and he worked it up, lifting her as he pulled up it to her waist.

Her shoes fell to the floor. He looked up at her, his lips curving in satisfaction as his fingers hooked in the top of her pantyhose. After he worked them down, his fingers immediately went to the waist of her panties, and before she knew it, they joined the pantyhose in a heap on the floor.

"There is something I've been dreaming about since that night, something I regretted not doing. Something I think you deserve Ms. Marlow." His voice was low and rough and it sent a cascade of shivers down her body. He went down on one knee, placing his hands partially beneath her rear end, and pulled her forward so she had to grab hold of the edge of the desk to balance herself.

He leaned forward, closed his eyes, and took a deep breath.

"Hmmm, lavender and aroused woman." He leaned forward and his tongue slid up her thigh, until he reached her feminine curls. He took another deep breath, and he exhaled, his hot breath warming her from her core. She had closed her eyes, trying to reign in the loss of control, when his tongue licked her from the bottom of her folds to the very top.

"Marlow, look at me." Marlow took a deep breath, and slowly opened her eyes. "You watch me, don't stop watching me. You tell me what you want."

He kneeled before her, practically at her feet in a submissive stance. A heady dose of power mixed with her arousal spiraled through her, pushing her to the edge.

"I want you to lick me. Like…like you did before," she said, her voice so husky she almost didn't recognize it.

He did as she asked, licking her as if savoring his favorite flavor of ice cream. Over and over, she watched as his tongue darted in between her folds, gliding in and out.

"Mmm, aroused, hot woman my favorite flavor. Anything else, Marlow?" he asked, still licking his lips as if savoring the taste of her as he waited for her answer.

"Yes, keep licking, but add your finger," she said, amazed by her boldness.

"Anything to make you happy, boss woman," Liam said, his head dipping between her legs again. He murmured something that sounded like "so wet," but she couldn't be sure because all the warmth from her body pooled between her legs, tension pulling her towards the pinnacle, trying to achieve that one thing to ease the ache.

"Yes, that's it. Oh, Liam, that feels so good." He added a second finger and continued to tease with his tongue and mouth.

"Oh, yes, Liam. Oh, my Lord, yes!" She leaned her head back, and spiked her fingers through his hair. He pulled her clitoris between his teeth and added another finger. His fingers glided in and out of her, slick with her juices. She moaned his name over and over as he devoured her. The soft bite of his teeth sent pulsating waves of heat through her blood. When she thought she would never reach the top that she would never satisfy the hunger, one little lick of his tongue against her clitoris sent her hurtling over the edge. She screamed his name, not caring about how loud she was, or who might hear. All she could think about were the delicious sparks running through her system.

She slumped over, her hands around Liam's neck, her chin on top of his head, allowing the warmth to surround her. His hand was still on her rear end. He rose just high enough to kiss her, and she tasted herself on his lips.

"I feel guilty," she said, realizing his knees had to be killing him. He had given her such a wonderful gift, while she gave him nothing in return.

"Why?" he asked, his voice rough and strained.

"Well, I, you know, and you didn't, Liam."

"You know?" he asked, humor lighting his voice and he rested his head against her belly while she toyed with the honey-colored strands of his hair. "You came, Marlow. And, it was one of the most erotic things I've ever seen or heard, but you don't need to worry about me."

She looked at him as he stood up, and her eyes were drawn to his fly, where a wet circle had formed.

"And you thought there was something wrong with you, woman. I haven't lost control and come in my pants since high school." He leaned forward, placed a kiss on her forehead, and then cradled it against his chest. "You are one hot woman, Marlow Jane Smith."

Her face heated. This man did things to her, caused her to lose control in every way when he was around her. She glanced around her office and then the horror of what she had just done slammed into like a sledgehammer. The ramifications of her actions stunned her.

Oh God, what had she been thinking?

Chapter 9

"This is not going to happen again, Liam."

The passion had drained out of her voice, the crisp tone had returned with a vengeance.

He pulled away from her and looked at her face. Her usually neat hair was a mess; strands had escaped the bun and fell in disarray around her face. Lips were swollen and red from kissing and she was tugging her bra and shirt back up. He was sure some of the redness on her face was from whisker burn.

Maybe he had carried it a little too far. Okay, he did carry it too far but he really hadn't intended to seduce the woman on her desk. He planned on teasing her, driving her crazy until she jumped his bones, but she responded so fast, there was nothing he could do to control himself. Knowing she'd never responded to anyone else that way made it even more of a thrill.

At least three months ago, she had never had anyone else who could do it for her. But, now, he just wasn't so sure. She had three months since Dallas to date. Hell, for all he knew, she had been going out every night with a different guy.

Because of that thought, his voice was a little harsher than he intended.

"What do you mean this can't happen again?"

She jumped, startled at the harsh tone.

"Liam, we're working together. We need to keep our relationship on a professional level."

"You're going out with Ken on Friday and you work with him." He crossed his arms over his chest and braced his feet wide apart, studying her as she finished dressing. Her trembling fingers made it hard for her to button up her blouse. Just like that, his anger dissolved and he was almost overwhelmed by tenderness for her.

"I told you, he's different," she said, as she scooted off the desk and pulled her skirt down. Just like that, his anger returned.

"Why is he different, Marlow? Because Daddy hand-picked him? You know," he said, anger and disgust mingling in his tone, "you might want to think for yourself one of these days. At the age of thirty, I would think you would be able to choose who you want to fuck, and not have to ask permission."

Her head snapped up and her eyes sparked with anger. "I don't choose you, so there's something wrong with me? Because I didn't pick some overgrown teenage jackass for a date, no wait," she said, "not even a date. A good screw. According to you, I screw someone because my Daddy picked him?" He shrugged as she started walking toward him in angry, little steps. Without her heels, she seemed so small.

"So, Ken, who has never lied about who he really was like you did so you could get laid, who's willing to be seen in public with me on a date and who treats me better than attacking me in my office is such a loser because…?" When he said nothing, she poked him in the chest, all the while advancing as he retreated towards the door.

"*You* lied to me about who you were, and *you* must think I'm too ugly to take on a date. And, to top it all off, *you* didn't even recognize me when you showed up here. And you're wondering if I'm letting my father choose my dates because I didn't choose you? *You're* such a good catch?"

Okay, when she put it that way, he did sound like a jack-ass. So maybe he forgot to tell her who he was. And, maybe, he should have remembered who she was when he met her again. But damn it he never said he was embarrassed to be seen with her. Most of the blood still had not returned to his brain, he had been enjoying the afterglow of one of the most erotic, sensual interludes in his life, and this impossible woman had to pick a fight with him, ruining the moment.

From the furious look on her face, there was no way he was even going to try to argue this one, though. That anger made her seem ten feet tall. She had backed him all the way to her door. Turning around, she grabbed his suit coat and threw it at him.

"What is this?" he asked, holding on to the anger because it was all he had. "Here's your coat, what's your hurry?"

"No, this is, take your coat and get the hell out of my office before I kick your ass out."

He looked down into her angry eyes, her lips drawn into an angry line and she was breathing heavily and realized he was getting hard again. Jesus, what was it about this woman, who knew nothing about enjoying the afterglow, that caused him to have a boner ninety-five percent of the time he was in her company?

She was nervous; he was hard. She was mad; he was hard. She was asleep; he was hard. Hell, at this point, he was worried about embarrassing himself at her funeral.

"Okay, but this isn't over, Marlow. There is no way you can experience what we just did and think you can just walk away from it." He angrily shoved his arms through the sleeves of his jacket, making sure he buttoned it up because he was not walking out there in front of Joey with a wet spot on his pants. She would know exactly what went on.

He grabbed Marlow by each of her upper arms and jerked her forward. Taking her lips in a bruising kiss, he allowed all the anger and passion to flow from him to her. She immediately, almost instinctively, he was sure, kissed him back. He drew back and released her arms and she almost stumbled trying to regain her balance.

Passion had crept back into her eyes and he knew at that moment, with a little work, he could have her again but he decided both of them needed time to think.

"You think about that, and other office activities when you're on your date this Friday night."

He shut the door behind him and tried to walk past Joey, hoping against hope she wouldn't comment on what went on behind that door.

"You should be a little more discreet," she said, eyeing him suspiciously.

"*You* should mind your own business."

"Yes, well, I'll reiterate my warning. You hurt her, I hurt you."

Irritated she even thought he would do something like that, he said, "I heard you the first time, Joey." He turned to walk out of the office, but her next statement stopped him.

"I thought you should have a little reminder. Just so you know, that woman in there lives and dies by her father's approval. Do you think she would recover from the embarrassment of getting caught in the middle of a nooner?"

He almost returned some sarcastic remark, but then what

she said sunk in.

Crap! He had been trying to gain her trust, letting her control things and because he lost control, he could have ruined everything.

Apparently noticing his realization, Joey said, "Yes. She would never forgive you. Next time, I suggest you keep it away from the office."

He nodded and headed out the door without saying another word. Liam knew he needed to be discreet. Marlow couldn't stand to lose face in front of her father, and he would never want to be a party to that. Being in constant contact with the woman was going to make that hard, though. He had to keep his hands off her while they were at the office, plain and simple.

* * * *

Friday morning, Marlow arrived early as usual, the office quiet and almost serene, except for the buzzing from the fluorescent light above that illuminated the hallway.

She unlocked her outer office, walked through and unlocked her door, making sure to close both of them behind her. Once she was sitting behind her desk, she looked through the upcoming promos they had with various food vendors. This time of year was busy. From Halloween to the Superbowl, the vendors had a lot of promos they liked to do.

She pulled out her reading glasses when someone knocked on her office door and then opened it. She was surprised to find Joey there.

"Good morning," Joey said with a smile. Dressed again in another bright color, fuchsia, she looked fit and wide-eyed awake, an unusual occurrence this early in the morning. "I just put some coffee on."

"You know I don't drink that much coffee, Joey."

"You look tired, honey. Having trouble sleeping *again?*"

"Joey! You know there's nothing going on between Liam and me."

"Well, at least not since Tuesday," she quipped and went back out into her office to probably get herself some coffee.

It had been four days since she lost her head and let Liam seduce her in her office. In the few meetings they'd had since then, Liam had been respectful and a bit formal, she should've been happy. But she wasn't happy at all. She missed having him flirt with her, saying impossible things to embarrass her and worse, she missed having him touch her.

Oh, every now and then, he would inadvertently brush her arm with his as he walked beside her, or maybe put his hand on the small of her back as he guided her through a doorway, but never a caress, never a lingering touch. The saddest thing was when she found herself walking closer to him, hoping his arm would brush against hers, or even sadder, walking slower to spend more time with him.

Since he hadn't been flirting with me, he had been flirting with everything that moved, including Joey. Most of the secretaries were half in love with him and the others wanted to adopt him. How could she blame them? She wanted to bring him home and wrap him up in the wedding quilt she had on top of her bed. Thinking of him in her bed made her blush but she couldn't stop the excitement zinging through her system.

Joey came back in, a coffee mug in each hand, kicking the door shut with her foot. Joey set a mug in front of her, and Marlow looked up at her with a dirty look. Joey ignored her and plopped down in the chair.

"I told you I don't want coffee," she said.

"I ignored you."

Marlow could argue with Joey but in the end, she knew she would lose. The only time Joey was this pushy was when she had something to talk about. She leaned forward, grabbed the mug, and took a sip.

"So, cut to the chase and tell me what this is all about."

"I think you need to break your date with Ken tonight."

"Listen, Joey, I know you don't like him. The truth is, I do. It's not going to be anymore than the two of us going to Abuelo's for dinner. It isn't really a date."

Joey snorted but remained silent for a few seconds. "You need to pay more attention to the hunk."

"Hunk?"

Joey's golden brown eyes narrowed. "Liam is perfect for you. You two would be good for each other."

"Joey, you know what he's like. He's just not into one woman."

"Have you seen him with anyone else? Something tells me there's more to his pursuit than you think."

"Joey, he's going to be here two more weeks, three tops. What he wants is someone to warm his bed while he's here. There isn't one good thing about it, Joey." Well other than if she was his personal bed warmer, she could snuggle up to him every night instead of reading progress reports until one in the morning.

"If all he wanted was a bed warmer, he could have that with no problem."

Now it was Marlow's turn to snort. She knew that was the truth. It had been one of the things keeping her awake at night. Marlow knew with his good looks and flirty personality, he could have any woman in the office, and she was sure, if he leaned that way, some of the men.

She pushed the morbid thought aside and took another sip of coffee, trying to avoid the conversation. Joey would never let her get away with telling lies. Marlow knew, if she didn't nip this conversation in the bud, she would end up crying in her coffee to Joey, telling her how she made a total fool out of herself the other day. How each night she fell asleep, wondering what to do about the aching for a man who really didn't want her, and waking up the next morning, cranky and out of sorts because she dreamt about him all night.

How, every now and then, she could still feel the ghost of his hands on her body; hear a whisper of his husky voice, hot against her ear.

"Are you going to your grandfather's this weekend?" Marlow asked, trying to change the subject. Guilt turned her stomach when she saw the shadow that passed over Joey's usually bright face. Joey's family put the dys in dysfunctional. She came from an extended family that rivaled the Kennedy's in size and wealth, and, even though she was estranged from them for the most part, they were constantly calling her with their family squabbles.

"Yes," she said. "I brought my bag and came in early, just in case I could leave before five."

"Sure. I have to leave early anyhow. Ken and I are going out earlier than planned since he's driving in early." She held her hand up when she noticed the mutinous look on Joey's face. "And, forget all of the arguments. I *am* going out with Ken tonight. Period. End of story."

Joey grumbled something under her breath that she would be home by eight and walked out of her office without another word.

* * * *

Sitting in the empty office Liam had claimed for himself, he wondered if he could actually die from spending the majority of his time with a hard-on. These past few days had been a lesson in pain, spending time with Marlow and not touching her. The dreams he had about her were so real, when he woke up, he would swear he could smell lavender on his sheets. And last night, he had his first wet dream since college.

What he should do is go and find him a woman. But as soon as the thought jumped to life, it died a fast death because the thought of using another woman as a substitute was just down right distasteful. A first for him.

He'd never had this burning, overwhelming need to own the women he slept with. Most knew the score and appreciated he made no demands on their time. Oh, a few of them hinted at serious relationships, taking things beyond the casual dinner and sex. But Marlow was different. In his mind, he was sure it was her resistance. He wasn't a grade-A bastard and had never forced a woman but the thought of someone he desired not wanting him…it was driving him insane. This desire, this unsatisfied, smoldering lust, would fizzle out after a few weeks, he was sure of it. All he had to do was get the woman to admit she wanted him.

But there was no way for him to test his theory if she wouldn't let him close to her. He hadn't touched her without her thinking it was inadvertent since that day in her office. Every now and then, they would be walking down the hall and he would brush up against her arm. That one little touch through four or five layers of clothing had him hard and wanting like a sixteen-year-old. It amazed him that he didn't just jump her in the hallway.

On top of it all, she had a date tonight with Ken, who apparently worked fast in San Angelo to get back up to Abilene for his Friday night date with Marlow. Well, who could blame the man?

He decided to get away from morbid thoughts, and walk down and talk to Ham. Although loud and sometimes irritating, he really liked Marlow's father. He was smart and he cared about the people who worked for him. The only problem he had with the man was the way he treated Marlow.

The woman had impressed him more than once in the past few days with her brain. Her ideas were fresh and she never minded when he made suggestions. She was open to new ideas, and she cared about saving jobs. Somewhere along the way, he had begun to really admire her, not only for that cute little body, but for that quick mind, too. Without thinking about where he was going, he turned in the direction of her office, and entered Joey's area, only to be almost plowed down by her.

"Oh, sorry," she said, picking up the overnight bag she had dropped.

"You have a fun weekend planned?" he asked. The curvy blonde had a different lunch date every day that week.

She laughed, but with no humor. "No, there's a family meeting and I've been summoned. But if you're looking for Marlow, she's already gone." She started down the hall to the elevator and he looked at his watch.

"She's gone?" he asked. "It's only four."

"Well," she said, struggling to punch the down button but it was hard because she was holding two bags, her purse and what looked like a briefcase of some sort, "Marlow knocked off early because of her *date*." He leaned forward and punched the down button. She gave him a brilliant smile. "Thanks. What are you going to do?"

Well, if she was gone, maybe he should go. "Hmm, maybe go by Betty Rose's, pick up dinner, go back to the hotel."

The doors slid open and they both got on. He punched the button for the lobby. She slanted him a look as she set her bags on the floor.

"Well, I would go for Mexican if I were you."

"Really? I haven't been to any of the Mexican restaurants here. Can you suggest one?"

One side of her mouth quirked, but before she could answer, the doors slid open and a couple of businessmen got on. Both of them gave her speculative looks, but she ignored them.

"Okay, I think you'd really like this place on South Fourteenth Street. It's in a shopping center on the left hand side. It's called Abeulo's and I highly recommend it. I also recommend you get there around six tonight."

As they reached the lobby, he bent and picked up a couple of the bags and she gave him an appreciative smile. The doors slid open and the men waited until she walked around them. The automatic doors slid open and an unseasonably warm wind smacked him in his face. Liam followed her to her car.

"If Marlow wants nothing to do with me, why are you doing this?" She stopped beside a little red convertible. "I thought you would take her side in this. She called you her best friend."

Joey turned to look at him, and he swore he saw her eyes tearing up. "She said that?" she asked, and he heard a suspicious sniffle.

Totally terrified of female tears like any other smart man, he said, "She also said she was going to fire you."

She let out a little laugh and her shoulders seemed to straighten, as if she had been relieved of some heavy burden.

"Well, she'd never really go through with it." She unlocked the trunk, and Liam put the two bags he carried and went after the odd looking briefcase, but she shook her head. "I keep this sucker close by." She unlocked the passenger door, and placed both her purse and her briefcase on the seat and shut the door. "Now are you going to change your mind about your choice of restaurants?" she asked.

"I'm not sure that would go over well."

She walked around to the driver side, opened the door, got in, started the engine, and shut the door.

"Jeez, it's hot today. I had to start the AC. Anyway, you need to crash the party. You need to save her from herself."

"What do you mean?"

She waved at a car driving by.

"She's going to be bored to tears tonight but she insists on going out with that man. Marlow thinks she knows what she needs, but she really doesn't."

"And you know what she needs?"

"No, but I do know what she doesn't need and she doesn't need someone as anal as she is. I hate to think what would happen if they married. Their children would be on Prozac by age five."

He grunted but didn't say anything. The truth was, he was having trouble getting past the idea of some other man with Marlow. Especially some other man having children with her. He stamped down the uncomfortable feeling. He didn't care whom she had children with. Really, he didn't.

"And get that look off your face. She's not going to like you coming there and attacking Ken. You use what got her to that hotel room the first night. It must have been something, because although she is a woman who has had a lot of dates, she never sleeps with them. Trust me on this."

"Why?"

"Why what?"

"Why are you trying to help me?" he asked, still totally baffled by this woman.

"I told you why. You'll be good for her. She needs a fling with a man who is fun. Ken is not fun."

"How do you know?"

"You've talked to the man. He's as nice as can be, but he's as interesting as a piece of bark. Well, I'm running a little late and I'm not in the mood for a confrontation. Go have Mexican. You'll thank me for it in the long run."

She drove away.

He shoved his hand in his pockets and walked to his car. Thinking about everything Joey said he had to admit Mexican food did sound good for dinner. He smiled as he anticipated Marlow's reaction. She would get that broom handle up her back and spit fire at him. As usual when Marlow came to mind, his groin tightened. Man, that woman turned him on, especially when she was mad which was odd because he usually didn't go for that type of passionate display from a woman.

Glancing at his watch, he realized he had just enough time to get to the hotel, shower, and change, and make it to the restaurant. He was in the mood for hot food and one hot woman.

Chapter 10

"So, do you think Jed is going to work out as the manager?" Marlow asked after she and Ken had been seated at their table.

Abuelo's was one of her favorite restaurants in town. With an open floor plan and ceramic tiled floor, the place was loud, making it difficult to have a conversation. They were seated at a table in the middle of the room, the scent of refried beans and sizzling fajitas drifting through the air. Mexican art decorated the stucco walls and Hispanic music played softly overhead. Marlow smoothed down the skirt of the soft cotton dress she had chosen to wear tonight because it matched the color of her eyes.

"He needs a little more training, but I think he'll be good. He was the third key, he's spent time night stocking and as a cashier. Jed is a little younger than I'd like, but he is enthusiastic."

She nodded in agreement. *Okay, now what.* Their conversation had been boring and stilted since he'd picked her up. Ken was usually easy to talk to. He had a great knowledge of music, books, and movies, he kept up on current events, and he was non-threatening.

Non-threatening? Is that what she thought of him? Why would she consider him non-threatening?

The waiter came by and took their drink orders. While she was studying the menu, she thought about her relationship with Ken. There were never any awkward moments and he respected her opinion. They both believed in schedules and planning, they even drove similar cars. But why would she classify him as non-threatening? She'd never used that term before when describing men.

Before she got too lost in her thoughts, Ken said, "Look, there's Liam."

She glanced up, alarmed, and saw he was looking toward the entrance and waving his hand, trying to get Liam's attention. "Ken, I'm really not sure he'd want to eat with us tonight."

"Don't be silly, Marlow. He doesn't know anyone in town."

Ken finally caught his attention, and Liam looked confused for a moment, then his face split into a smile dimples and all. Ken motioned Liam to join them, and Liam sauntered over.

"Imagine running into you two here," he said.

Marlow studied him and couldn't help the slow shiver of warmth spreading through her body at the sight of him. He'd changed into the same green shirt he wore the night they met and he was wearing jeans. Jeans that looked soft from repeated washings and fit him to a T. They hugged his lean hips and legs and the huge belt buckle he wore drew attention to the way they cupped his sex.

Her eyes traveled back up to his face and he gave her a smile that told her he knew what she'd been thinking. Her face burned with embarrassment. She quickly glanced over at Ken but he was busy telling Liam to take a seat.

Liam gave her a little satisfied smirk as he sat down and she realized this meeting had been planned. But how was that possible? She didn't tell anyone but Joey where she was going for dinner.

Joey! She was going to kill her! No! She was going to fire her and *then* she'd kill her. Liam was chatting amiably with Ken like there was nothing wrong. He gave himself away though because every few seconds, he slanted her a look out of the corner of his eye.

The waiter came and took their order and Marlow sat back in her chair, her arms crossed over her breasts, staring at the two men as they chatted about anything from west Texas weather, to the problems they were having at Smith's.

"I'm really glad to run into you, Campbell. I thought I'd have to wait until Monday to talk to you."

"I won't be in," Liam said. "I'm leaving Sunday afternoon and I'll be out of town until late Monday." He glanced over at her. "It's my mom's birthday and I never miss it." Both of those dimples appeared and she softened, just a bit. She took a drink of water in an effort to calm her nerves and ignore the mushy feelings that rose every time she heard his seductive voice. "I love to celebrate birthdays, don't you *Marlow?*"

She choked on her water and he reached over and patted her back. "Are you alright?" Mock innocence shone in his eyes.

"Oh, Marlow's a real trooper," Ken said.

Well, that was definitely not a roses and champagne kind of compliment. Good Lord, he made her sound like an Army recruit.

The waiter returned with their meals and more chips. Marlow loved Mexican food the hotter the better. Deciding she would deal with Liam later, she dug into her cheese enchilada and almost hummed in pleasure. The flavor of the hot spices mixed with the melted cheese exploded in her mouth. She took another bite, and couldn't help but hum this time.

Liam had grown silent and she glanced in his direction. He had stopped eating and was staring at her. All the moisture in her mouth evaporated as his gaze flicked to her lips and she couldn't help but lick them in reaction. His eyes darkened.

Ken continued to drone on, while Liam concentrated on her lips as she licked the last of the salt off them. Heat zinged through her body as his eyes followed her tongue. She cleared her throat and his eyes shot to hers. Grabbing his glass of tea, he drained the glass, setting it down with a thud on the ceramic tabletop. He looked away and took a deep breath. After a few moments, his jaw muscles relaxed but he still didn't look in her direction. Instead, he concentrated on eating.

She took a slow breath and released it, trying to ease the tension in her body. Little sparks of electricity still coursed through her. She shifted in her chair, trying to ease the warm ache between her legs. All the man did was look at her for heaven's sake!

Several moments later, Liam seemed to regain control and he picked up a conversation string with Ken, who had been talking to himself for the past few minutes.

"If you could do one thing with Smith's, what would you do?" Liam asked Ken.

"Oh, I would probably invest more time and money in the bigger markets. The consumers in places like Dallas and Houston are willing to pay more money for things. They'll spend extra money on ready-made foods because of the convenience."

Marlow suppressed the urge to snort. That sounded exactly like something her father said the last time they argued. Both Ken and her father refused to listen to her warnings.

"Hmm," Liam said as the waiter placed their entrees in front of them. "Marlow, what would you do?"

She looked up at him, surprised he wanted her opinion, but then she really shouldn't have been. In the past few days, Liam had asked her opinion about a lot of things and had always listened. He didn't always agree with her viewpoint, but he acted as if he respected it, nonetheless.

Marlow cleared her throat. "Well, I think emphasizing those markets will hurt Smith's in the long run. There's a lot of competition for the middle-upper class consumer and with our problems, sinking money into that market is going to drain our assets."

He mulled that over for a few minutes, as he tasted his enchilada. "So you would pull out of those markets?"

"No. That would be stupid. We're still making money in them and building in that market a few years down the road would be a good idea. But we expanded too fast and Daddy doesn't believe in using credit to build. I agree but it has drained our resources. Small improvements in our smaller markets would help bring back some of the customers who've left us for the other grocers who have remodeled or built new stores. It would also entice newer, younger customers."

"This is where Marlow and I differ in opinion. I think there's no way we can compete with these super stores the discount chains are opening," Ken said.

"If we can't compete with them in towns like Abilene,

then how can we compete with them in Dallas?" she asked.

"More consumers," he said. "Besides, these hokey little towns have very little to offer any chain store." Her blood boiled and her head almost exploded. She hated the condescending view Ken had about places like Abilene. People in these towns may not have been as sophisticated as people in places like Dallas, but they had every right as consumers to a choice. Before she could voice her opinion, Liam interrupted.

"Hmm, both good arguments. I have my brother Heath working on some market research. I tend to side with Marlow, though. The backbone of this company was, and still is, the little town." Her anger dissolved and guilty warmth invaded her at his agreement. "The only way to survive without them, is to invest heavily in the bigger cities. And to do that, you have to have unlimited resources. Or, you need to get extended credit. I know Ham doesn't like to use it."

"He's considering it to hit the seventy-five store mark," Ken said, and the glow from Liam's approval plummeted into icy pain.

She looked at Ken, who didn't even know he'd hurt her with that one comment, and fought back the tears. Her father was considering a major change in company policy and hadn't even talked to her about it. He was going to build on credit for the first time, listening to a man that didn't even have an MBA or the experience in the store she did. A lump formed in her throat but she swallowed it.

"If you'll excuse me, I need to use the restroom." She grabbed her purse and stood.

Ken kept eating but Liam stood and looked at her with concern. If he showed even one bit of kindness to her, she would fall apart right here. She would break down and cry like a baby. That was something she hadn't done in years, and she refused do it now. She gave him a small smile and hurried to the restroom, hoping to make it before she started to cry.

* * * *

Marlow hurried off to the restroom and Liam couldn't help but be concerned. The look of pain in those big violet eyes had cut him deep. Ken, the jackass, sat there eating his meal, and continued to talk about the need for building more stores.

Liam really wanted to hurt the man. He'd always had what his mother called a gallant streak, but this was different. This was bone deep. He needed to see Ken in pain. The idiot had no idea he hurt Marlow. This woman, who lived her life to please her father, had just been told, in a horrible way, her father had confided in another person. Not because he was more qualified. Marlow had more years in the store than he did and she had an MBA. No, because he was a man.

Liam had never had to worry about acceptance in his family. His parents were pleased with his success, but then again, they would be happy if he was a ditch digger. As long as he and his brother were happy, they didn't care what they did. Well, his mother had mentioned grandchildren. But other than that, they were happy.

Marlow, on the other hand, had never had acceptance from her father, or her mother, for that matter. Several times at dinner the other night, her mother had made reference to Marlow's intelligence hindering her chances of finding a man. Her father would never take her opinions seriously, unless a man backed her up.

He was about to get up and check on her, when she walked across the floor toward them. Her eyes were a little red but other than that, she looked fine.

Not for the first time that evening, Liam admired the way she dressed. He had gotten used to the ugly, boxy suits she wore to work. The blue dress she wore almost matched the color of her eyes, making them appear even larger. It was made of some soft cotton fabric that clung to her breasts then flared out at the waist, unfortunately, covering her legs. For the first time since Dallas, Marlow wore her hair down, but it was not the riot of curls he was sure Joey designed. No, her mass of ebony hair was bone straight and almost reached her waist. He would never be able to see her hair and not want to drag his fingers through it, or think about having it drape across his chest as she leaned down to kiss him good morning. The thought of spending a morning rolling around in bed with Marlow sent a shock of heat to his groin. He shifted in his chair, trying to ease the tightness of his jeans.

She approached the table and he stood and pulled her chair out for her. The jackass was finishing off his tea. He pushed her chair in, leaned next to her and whispered in her ear, "Are you alright?" She looked up, a little surprised from the expression on her face, and nodded without saying a word.

"Marlow," Ken said, "I was wondering if you minded if I dropped you off early. I wanted to get to the office and catch up on some work."

Before she could even think of an answer, Liam said, "I'll be happy to take you home, Marlow." He paused because the waiter brought the check. He grabbed the check and said, "I'll pay for this one. I can write it off as a business expense." Marlow's eyes narrowed in suspicion. "I'll even leave the *tip*, unless you'd like to, Marlow. I've noticed you are a good tipper." Her face flushed red with anger or embarrassment, he wasn't sure which, but he was thinking it was the first option when those blue eyes turned almost violet in anger. *Oh, yeah, she was mad.* And she looked like she recovered from the earlier conversation. Why it was so important to him she wasn't so sad, was beyond him. He never wanted to see any woman upset, but seeing this woman almost break down in tears, cut him deep. Maybe it was because he knew this wasn't a woman who broke down that often.

"Well," her totally oblivious date said, "you have a good night. You don't mind Liam taking you home, do you, Marlow?" he asked as they headed out the door.

She shook her head and he leaned over and gave her a totally platonic peck on the cheek that had Liam seeing red and his hands itching to smack the jackass. He watched Ken walk away and then turned to face Marlow. Her eyes were spitting blue fire, she had her hands on her hips, and she was breathing heavily. Her chest rose with each breath, and the blood drained from his brain.

Jesus! She was magnificent! Excitement skittered down his spine. All he had to do was find a way to get her to release all that passion, preferably in bed with him.

* * * *

"What the hell was that all about?" she asked.

"Couldn't let the jackass have a date with my girl, now could I?"

Marlow's pulse jumped when he referred to her as his girl but she stamped it down. To put some space between them, she decided to find his car. She spotted his baby blue convertible Mustang a couple rows over and headed in that direction.

Her head was pounding with unreleased anger, and her heart still hurt from her father's slight. She wanted to go home and curl up with the new romance novel she'd bought the day before. And chocolate. She needed chocolate in the worst way. She was going to eat a gallon of double chocolate fudge ice cream, right out of the carton.

She reached his car and had to wait for him to catch up. He came up and stood beside her. When their eyes met, she recognized a trace of apology in his. But, before she could soften toward him, she remembered his crack about tipping, the beast!

He reached around her to unlock her door. His arm brushed against hers and she shivered. He unlocked it and held it open and closed it for her once she was seated. She took a few calming breaths before he got into the car. As he sat down in his seat, the leather upholstery creaked. His sandalwood cologne, mixed with the smell of outdoors, filled the interior, overpowering her senses.

He started the car and put it in reverse, accidentally brushing his hand against her thigh. Her breath caught in her throat and she looked over at him, but he gave no sign of recognition. The truth was, it had barely been a touch, but it had her body tingling and her heart beating hard against her ribs.

The ride to her apartment was uncomfortably quiet. Each time he shifted, his hand brushed against her knee or thigh. Each slight touch sent a flood of vibrations down to her toes. She knew, as soon as they got to her apartment, he would try to work his way inside and into her bedroom.

Or maybe not. Maybe he just wanted to show her something about being in charge tonight. Maybe he wanted to get back at her for kicking him out of her office. She really didn't know, but she realized his lack of attention meant he had found someone new.

That would really be for the best. It would be best if he were to go on his merry way, giving multiple orgasms to everyone else in the office. As soon as the thought appeared, she had to swallow past the lump of pain in her chest. Suspicious of any kind of feeling associated with any man, especially this one, she pushed it aside. Quick, hot affairs weren't her cup of tea, and that was all Liam had to offer.

He parked in visitor's parking and got out, rounding the hood and opened her door. She looked up at him. He smiled and the street light behind him cast shadows to that smile, adding a sinister quality to it. A shiver raced down her spine as she placed her hand in his proffered one.

"I guess I'm supposed to ask you in for a nightcap," she said sarcastically. He followed silently behind her and when she reached her door, she turned to find him studying her. Before she could say anything, he answered her question.

"I would love one but the truth is, you still hold a grudge against me because of the other day. I've kept my word and my distance."

Her cheeks burned because she knew he was right and she was accusing him for no reason.

"I'm sorry, it's just you kept touching my thigh and my knee in the car and it was driving me crazy."

His eyes widened a bit and a look of real confusion marked his features. "What do you mean?" he asked, looking completely bewildered. Her cheeks burned even brighter when she realized those touches didn't mean as much to him as they did to her.

"Never mind." She turned to unlock her door. He

touched her shoulder, just a simple touch, but it sent a chorus of vibrations zinging throughout her body. What was is about this man that made her melt with just one touch?

It was his first real touch since the office incident and she leaned into it.

"Marlow, I would like to come in and talk. I promise I won't try anything."

And that was a plus? His fingers started to massage her shoulder and all she could think about right then were those hands on her body. "Having someone to talk to would be a good thing right now."

She didn't say anything for a moment or two. Drained and hurt, she really wanted to just curl up with that book, eat chocolate, and forget about tonight. His hand continued to caress her shoulder, easing the tension. She closed her eyes, enjoying the touch of his fingers.

"Marlow," he whispered in her ear, "you need someone to talk to. I promise that's all we'll do."

His voice, warm and tender, broke down the last of her defenses. She sighed, releasing the last of the tension.

"Why not? Joey is out of town and I feel the need to vent."

Chapter 11

Liam couldn't believe he'd made it into Marlow's apartment. He followed her down the hallway to a cozy living room done in soft blues and greens. Against one wall, a small TV sat on top of an antique table. There was a comfy looking couch and loveseat and a table littered with candles in various stages of life. A small dinette sat off to one side and he could see a faint light from the doorway to the right and figured it was the kitchen. Everything was in its place, even the throw pillows on the sofa looked like they had been placed in just the right spots.

"Nice," he said, amazed his voice was even and not rough with the lust churning his gut. When she'd made the comment about touching her thigh, it took every ounce of control he had to make sure she didn't know just how pathetic he was. He was a thirty-three-year-old man who, to satisfy some teenaged-style lust, had to brush his hand "inadvertently" against her thigh. He was like some out of control adolescent, copping a feel off one really hot student body president.

And what a body. He admired the way her dress clung to her breasts.

"What would you like?" she asked, her soft, cool voice

washing over him. For a moment, his hormone-soaked brain sputtered and then images of exactly what he wanted from her blazed across it. The heaviness in his groin increased but he realized she was heading to the kitchen.

She opened the fridge and peered inside. "I'm afraid I don't have much, but I do have some orange juice, some milk and tea. That's about it, unless you'd like some water or coffee."

She was standing in front of him, looking cool and composed, except, even in the pale light from the fridge, he could see her pulse fluttering in her throat and she kept pushing her hair behind her ears. He knew he could probably press his suit and have little Ms. Marlow on the floor for dessert, but he decided against it. For the first time in his life, he was going to put something in front of the sexual side of a relationship.

This woman had been through the ringer the past couple days and he couldn't use that as a means to get her into bed, or on the floor.

"I think I'd like some water after all that hot food tonight," he said, smiling at her.

She gave him a small, wary smile, nodded, and then filled a glass with water and ice. She fixed herself some tea and then motioned for him to go to the living room. She joined him and sat on the couch, he was on the loveseat, both of them sipping their drinks in silence.

"So, you had no idea your father was talking about buying stores on credit?"

He could see her pain flash but she quickly masked it.

"No, I had no idea. I wish he would talk these things over with me, but he seems to think I don't know what I'm doing. He won't ever take me seriously, no matter what I do." She took a shaky breath. "Oh, that sounded pathetic."

Anger boiled in his blood. The man could at least listen to her. "No, what's pathetic is your father listening to the refrigerator."

A little laugh bubbled out of her and he smiled. He was really the pathetic one. That one sad little laugh made him feel like king of the world. "No, I'm used to him disregarding my opinion." She held up her hand to stop his argument. "No, really. What bothered me the most was he talked to Ken about it, without even mentioning it to me."

"How do you know that?"

"I know what my father discussed with me, Liam."

"No, how do you know if he talked about it with Ken?"

Her eyes widened then narrowed in concentration. "What reason would he have to lie to me, Liam?"

He shrugged, happy he'd possibly come up with something to wedge between Marlow and Moore. "I'm not sure. Do you think he sees you as a threat?"

"That's silly," she scoffed. "My father will never take me seriously."

"I don't understand why you stay."

She sighed and looked down into her glass. "It's hard to explain. I just want to please him, that's all." Her voice had grown smaller and smaller as the conversation progressed and he didn't like it. Where was the lady who told him thanks but no thanks? He had to do something to get her fire lit, so he said something he knew would irritate her.

"So, have you slept with him?" he asked, amazed at the green monster that reared its head. He had meant to get her riled, not himself.

Her head snapped up so quickly, he was amazed it didn't

snap off. Anger brought a flush to her cheeks and icy fire to those blue eyes. "What right do you have to ask me that?" she asked, her voice low and angry.

"Every right. I'm your lover."

"You were my paid escort."

"I never got paid," he said.

"I left a tip."

"Yeah, and judging by the tip, I was pretty damn good." He didn't add he still carried the hundred-dollar bill folded up in his wallet.

Her gasp of outrage filled the room and before he knew it, he was covered with tea, ice, and all.

"Crap! Get up!" she yelled. "Look what you made me do, you idiot!"

He stood, only because he knew the tea would stain her couch. She ran to the kitchen. Liam grabbed up the pieces of ice he could find and moved one of the pillows, trying to save it from the spreading tea.

Marlow rushed back with a roll of paper towels. He reached for them, but she just flew past him to the couch.

"I knew I never should have allowed you in."

"Now what is that supposed to mean?" he said, picking up the roll where she had dropped it. He unrolled some towels, ripped them off and began patting himself down.

"That means anytime I'm around you, things like this happen."

He looked up from his chore and eyed her suspiciously. "Things like this?"

"You just can't let things go. You just keep pushing and shoving until I lose my temper." She heaved a sigh. "I don't do it that often. Look at Dallas, and my office, look at what you make me do!"

Anger rolled inside him, until he looked at her face. The self-recrimination he saw there sent a shock of pain to his chest. Liam didn't want this proud woman to hate herself. He dropped the paper towels and took a step toward her, causing her to take a step back.

"Marlow, sweetheart, there's nothing wrong with what happened between us. You're a woman with a healthy sexual appetite, that's all." He watched her swallow convulsively, and then asked, "You don't think there's anything wrong with that, do you?"

"No," she said, avoiding looking him in the eye. "No, it's not that, it's that I don't like the feeling."

"The feeling?" he asked completely confused. He smiled and then said, "You sounded like you liked it."

Another little bubble of a laugh sprang from her. Her face flushed a little. "Don't do that."

"Do what?"

"Oh, you know what you do. You make me laugh, thinking I'll forget I'm mad at you."

"It works? I thought you stayed mad at me, except when you're screaming my name."

"Stop it. Your mother would be ashamed of you."

"She's actually very proud of me."

"Really." She crossed her arms beneath her breasts. The dress she was wearing showed no cleavage whatsoever, but the action plumped up her breasts, making them more visible underneath the denim material.

Besides, he knew what they looked like. They were small and pert just perfect for his hands with little pink nipples that pebbled at the softest caress. At that moment, all the blood drained from his brain to another part of his anatomy. He shifted, hoping she didn't notice the bulge in his jeans.

"Let's get back to this feeling you have when you're with me. Does it happen to move you to tear off my clothes and jump my bones?"

She snorted. "You wish."

"Oh, honey, I do more than wish, I dream nightly of that." And just like that, the air between them thickened. Marlow walked away from him, and he could see her visibly trying to gather her composure. She kept her back to him, but he could feel the memories of their lovemaking wash over both of them. The air grew taut with sexual awareness, and both of them held their breaths.

"You do not," she said, turning around abruptly. "Why would I, probably the most inexperienced woman you've slept with, be starring in your dreams?" Her voice had taken on a slight edge.

"I don't know, really," he replied honestly. "All I know is it's been three months and you're the only woman I want." Her eyes widened slightly but she kept quiet. He walked toward her. "Here I was, a man purported to be a gigolo," he said, smiling when she blushed again, "and I was spending every night at home, thinking about some sexual bombshell with long, black hair and violet eyes." Her mouth formed a little "O" but no sound came out. "There's a reason I exploded like I did in your office. I'm not used to going without for that long."

Her eyes narrowed. "I don't believe that, Liam."

He tamped down the anger boiling to the top when she made the statement. "You think I don't have any discretion, do you?"

"You slept with me, and you didn't even know me."

"First of all, we didn't do a lot of sleeping. Second of all, there was no way in hell I could let you go back to your hotel room to celebrate your birthday alone."

The memory of the hotel room, the many places they made love, the way she moaned his name, crashed through his system, causing his groin to tighten further. He had to gain control of his libido before he embarrassed himself again.

"Now tell me how you feel around me. Explain this feeling you've been talking about."

* * * *

She walked toward the sliding glass door, looked out, but didn't really see anything. The things he had said had wormed into her heart, softening her just a bit. But the years of dating men after position, and not love, had taught her a lot. Oh, he wasn't after her to gain any favor with her father, all he wanted was sex.

Excitement tingled down her spine before she could do anything to stop it. "I don't like losing control."

"Explain this, losing control," he requested softly. His voice was closer and she could almost feel his energy reaching out to her.

She swallowed. "I don't like feeling out of control. And that's how I feel around you."

"Marlow," he said and she could hear the smile in his voice, feel the warmth of his body behind her. "You have to know that isn't true."

She twirled around, angered he would make light of her dilemma, but instead of the mocking look she expected, she found him staring down at her with a smile full of warmth and tenderness that did funny things to her insides.

"Isn't true?" she asked, her voice a hoarse whisper. She could smell his aftershave and the fresh smell of man mixed with the night air.

He took her hand in his, entwining his fingers with hers. "You have to know I'm the one lost here. I'm a man used to getting what I want. Whether it's in business or my personal life, I'm used to pursuing what I want. The truth is, I'm not sure wanting you is such a good thing." He lifted her hand and began to kiss her fingers. Just soft little pecks, really, but each soft touch of his lips sent shivers racing through her, warming her from the inside out. He took her hand in between his.

"For the first time in my life, I want something I'm not sure I can get. Nothing I do or say seems to change your mind about me. And at the end of the day, I'm tired of restraining myself and the sad thing is, I'm not really sure you want me."

She looked at him, nonplussed. Not want him? "Liam, you have to know I do."

"Well," he said, a small smile curving his lips, "you don't want to want me. Why not, Marlow?"

"I don't like the feelings you elicit."

He studied her for a second. "You don't like being out of control?"

"No. Liam, in my world, everything has a place." He looked at her, confused for a second and then she continued. "I don't like uncontrollable feelings."

"But, Marlow, you control things here."

"No I don't." She tried to pull her hand out of his. He looked down at their joined hands, sighed, and then let go.

"Yes you do. It's amazing what kind of control you have, honey. I'm a man who rarely abstains, but since that night together three months ago, I haven't had an appetite for another woman. I kept returning to that same club, sitting there like a pathetic puppy, waiting for you to show up." The confession was not an easy one for him to make, she could tell. "Then, by accident, I find you again, and you hold me off. The one woman who has haunted my dreams and my daytime hours and you make me wait. And so I do. I wait for you to decide."

He took her hand and placed it on his chest, his hand over hers. She could feel the beating of his heart, hard against his chest, keeping perfect time with hers. "I ache for you, woman, and you turn me away," he said, moving her hand down his chest, past his abdomen, to his groin. He released her hand but she pressed against him, reveling in the hot, hard length of his penis. She looked up at him. "I spend ninety-five percent of my day half-cocked, waiting for you to tell me you want me. You have no idea just how much control *you* have over me, Marlow."

She caressed him through his pants and he leaned his head back, closing his eyes, and groaned. As she moved her hand up and down, she watched him swallow. Triumph sped through her system, mixing with the passion, churning her emotions. She looked down at her hand on the front of his jeans. His hand whipped down and caught hers. She looked up, surprised, and found him with a painful smile on his face.

"You keep doing that, woman, and we'll have a repeat of what happened in your office."

Power pulsed through her blood, giving her courage. She smiled up at him, and unbuttoned and unzipped his jeans. He swallowed again, his green eyes dark with uncontrollable lust as she pushed aside the denim.

She reached inside expecting to feel cool, clean cotton, but instead felt his hard, hot skin.

"Turn about is fair play, Marlow," he said, but it ended on a gasp as her hand encircled his penis. She slid her hand down to the base, feeling the crisp, curling hair brush against the back of her hand, then slid it back up, gliding her thumb over the tip of it. Sticky hot discharge dampened her hand and she knew just how close he was. The slow roll of desire that had knotted her belly unfurled, spreading warmth throughout her body.

Slowly, she slid her hand down his erection again, all the way to the base and the ragged moan that escaped him empowered her to conquer her doubts. She licked her lips, sliding her hand back up and over the top, feeling that stickiness again. She spread the thick liquid around the head of his penis. Marlow worried her bottom lip as she wondered if it would taste sweet or salty.

He groaned. "You're killing me here, Marlow." She didn't look up because she knew she would lose her nerve. Without thinking about it one second more, she dropped to her knees in front of him. "No, Marlow, baby, you have got to slow down. You do that, I'm not going to last."

She didn't say a word and refused to look up at him. Marlow bent her head forward and touched her tongue to just the tip, licking a bit of the liquid. She tasted him, saltiness, and man, and her nipples tightened and the dampness between her legs increased. He reached for her head, at first, to probably stop her, but he ended up clenching his fingers in her hair.

She leaned back, just a couple of inches and looked up at him as he looked down, passion shimmering in his eyes, his chest moving rapidly with each breath he took. Marlow unbuttoned his shirt, and then trailed her hand down his stomach and past his huge erection. Curious, she cupped his testicles, squeezing and measuring them, eliciting another groan from him.

She looked up at him again and smiled. Marlow kept her eyes locked on his as she leaned forward and took him into her mouth. She twirled her tongue around the tip, drinking in his essence and reveling in the power she had discovered. Then she licked down his length and back again. She sucked, and then twirled her tongue around his broad head, repeating the motions over and over. His fingers gently massaged her scalp as he whispered encouragement. He was almost incoherent at times, but his deep voice gave her confidence. She cupped his rear end, one cheek in each hand, trying to pull him closer. Closing her eyes she quickened her pace, sucking and licking, needing to help him, bring him to the end.

He shouted her name as he exploded, the warm liquid sliding down her throat. She leaned back looking up at him, and he leaned against the back of the sofa. Her body pulsed with unspent desire, but she didn't care. He took hold of her arm, pulling her up and into a hug. She rested her head on his shoulder. He kissed her temple and whispered her name. She shivered as the sound of her name from his lips washed over her.

At that moment, everything faded away, all her reservations, all her problems became nothing. Marlow realized she'd stepped over the line and offered him something she'd never really offered to another man in her life: her heart.

Chapter 12

Every muscle in Liam's body resembled melted butter. Never in his life had he been so relaxed. He was thankful he had the back of the sofa to lean against otherwise he would have been flat on his ass on the floor. Passion still lingered in Marlow's eyes.

As he raised his hands to cup her face, his hands shook. *No wonder*. He had wanted her to come out of her shell but he never guessed the woman would drop to her knees in front of him and use her sweet mouth.

He kissed her mouth, softly, gently, and then moved to her cheek.

"You're one up on me, Marlow," he said, trying to tease but the draining passion made his voice too hoarse to sound jovial. His hands were still shaking as he moved her to his side, slinging his arm over her shoulders. He pulled his pants up with his other hand and glimpsed his boots. His pants were around his ankles and his boots were still on. Jesus, the woman really did have him under her control. "I need some rest, woman."

She laughed, one of those carefree laughs he loved, and nodded. Her arm sneaked around his waist, and they walked together down the hall to her bedroom. The light was off but the one in the hall showed a queen-sized bed, covered with pillows and he almost stumbled to get there. He fell onto the bed and Marlow helped him out of his boots and turned to leave but he grabbed her arm and growled, "Stay." She got into bed beside him, snuggling up to his side as he drifted off to sleep.

A long time later, Liam awoke, hotter than Texas in July. He looked around the bedroom, noticing the difference from his hotel room and remembered he was in Marlow's apartment in her bed. Then he remembered what had happened, how she dropped to her knees in front of him. His groin thickened when the silky strands of her hair slid across his stomach. A smile spread across his face. He was going to get to spend the night.

"That sure is a self-satisfied smile you have there." The hallway cast shadows around the room, but he could still make out her face, her blue eyes sparkling up at him.

"Well, not *self*-satisfied," he said, and she smacked him on the chest and then rubbed the spot. He chuckled. "I'm sorry."

"Sorry, for what?" she asked. Her fingers were tangling through his chest hair.

"Hmmm. Oh, falling asleep." She ducked her head and rested it on his chest. "Why don't you wear your hair down more often?" He slipped his fingers though a few strands of the ebony silk.

"It's so thick and heavy. It sometimes gives me a headache from the weight of it. Joey's been trying to talk me into cutting it for a year now."

"I thought you kept it up because it would get in the way. Or maybe because you thought it made you look too sexy."

She raised her head off of his chest and looked at him as if he were crazy. "You seem a little preoccupied by my hair."

"Yeah, and various other body parts," he said, as he slipped his hand up to cup her breast. She hummed and closed her eyes. "But, I have a few fantasies about this hair. I would have never guessed it was so straight."

She leaned closer, encouraging his caress and even through the soft cotton material, he could feel her hardening nipple. He loved the way the woman responded to him. At that moment, he needed to see her naked. He wanted to explore every part of that body. The pretty pink nipples, the smooth rounded belly, those gorgeous thighs. Hell, he wanted to explore her tiny arched feet and he'd never been a foot man.

Liam increased the pressure, just a bit, and she collapsed in bed. He leaned down and touched his lips to hers. They were cool, soft, and wet. She immediately opened her mouth in invitation and he almost shouted in triumph. Chasing after her had been a real turn on, but her surrender was so much sweeter.

He unbuttoned the top of her dress and slipped his hand inside, feeling cool, smooth flesh. Heat pooled in his groin, pulling his testicles tight when he realized she wasn't wearing a bra. Her nipple was pebbled and straining against his hand. He rose up and said, "Marlow, once again I have to point out you're not quite the girl I thought you were." Her lips curved into a small smile, robbing him of thought.

"I often go without a bra, Liam, there isn't much to hold up." He could hear the wry amusement in her voice. Then what she said had an impact. Any blood that had been left in his brain now headed south, racing to his dick.

"You mean, you go to work without a bra on?" he asked, his voice sounding hoarse, even to him. She didn't answer immediately, and he removed his hand from her breast and she moaned in protest.

"Yes, most of the time." She grabbed his hand and put it on

her breast again. He chuckled at the move, but rolled her nipple between his thumb and forefinger just the same. She let loose a ragged moan, and his need to see her naked increased tenfold. He removed his hand from her breast, drawing a protest from her but he jumped off the bed and stripped out of his clothes, very aware her gaze never left his body. He grabbed her hand and pulled her out of bed, yanked her dress over her head, and stripped her panties off and threw them over his shoulder.

She laughed. A laugh so husky and sexy it made him think the shy little woman from dinner and this one could not be one and the same. But he was wrong. They were one in the same, shy but sexy, inexperienced but so damn good.

He looked his fill. Marlow was tiny but she had one of the sweetest bodies he'd ever seen. Her hair spilled over her shoulders, accentuating the paleness of that smooth, ivory skin. Her breasts were small and perfect, tipping up ever so slightly with their sweet little rosebud nipples puckered, waiting for him to taste them.

His eyes traveled down to her stomach, rounded just a bit. Then he looked down further and saw the black curls at the apex of her thighs. He thought of what lay hidden within those curls. Those sweet, pink lips that had tasted so honey sweet, and unbelievably, his dick hardened.

He smoothed his hand on her stomach and marveled at the contrast of his tanned hand against her alabaster skin. Her stomach muscles contracted at the first contact, and he slid his hand up to cup her breast.

"I've never seen such wonderful breasts before."

"Liam, I just want to make sure you understand one thing." Her voice was small and vulnerable. "I just want you to promise me you won't lie to me. You don't have to fib about all of my attributes. I know I'm not the most beautiful or successful woman you've ever been with, but that's all right. I just want you to be truthful."

"Marlow, you have to know you have one amazing body." She didn't say anything and all the lust that had boiled beneath his skin simmered down. He wanted her to understand he never played games with compliments. Without warning, he leaned over and turned on the light. Both of them winced but he looked down and the wariness he saw on her face cut him to the core. *What kind of jackasses had she dated?*

"Marlow, when I give you a compliment, I mean it." She still looked unconvinced, but he wouldn't let this go. He leaned back on one of his elbows, using his free hand to stroke her breast. "These are just perfect. I have pretty big hands, but your breasts fit perfectly." He slid his palm over it and just left it there. "See, just enough. Not too much, not too little. And your nipples," he said, moving his palm lightly over it, "they pucker at the slightest touch. Have they always been so responsive?" She didn't say anything, so he looked up and waited. She shook her head and he felt like he had been handed the key to the city. He looked down at her breasts again, his mouth watering.

"You know, another thing I like about you is your belly." One of those silly, disbelieving laughs he loved bubbled out. "It's true, you know." He moved down the bed, positioning himself between her legs. He could feel her moist heat on his chest. Kissing her stomach, he breathed in her lavender scent. "It's not all muscular like so many women today. No. It's rounded just a bit, just like a woman should be."

"Liam," she said.

"Now," he said, moving even further down, "this is beyond

anything I've ever seen. You have the smoothest, most beautiful skin I've ever seen, Marlow. But, down here," he said, leaning forward and breathing in the scent of her musky arousal, "there's the white skin, all that black hair and," he said, sliding his finger in between her folds, "these pouty lips." Her moan let him know she was getting the message.

He dragged his finger from the bottom up to the top, loving the dampness that seeped out. Liam slid one finger in, massaging his thumb against her swollen clitoris. Lust seared through him as he watched it swell even further.

"Liam," she moaned, and she pulled on his hair. "Liam, come up here," she said. He hesitated for a second, looking around for his pants. "Top drawer of my nightstand."

He pulled it open, fumbled around until he felt the foil, and pulled out a strand of condoms. Before he could contemplate what she was doing with so many, she grabbed them out of his hand, ripped one off and tore it open. She was rolling it down his penis and shoving him on his back before he could think.

She looked at him. In the soft light from her bedside lamp, he could see the passion in her eyes. He rolled her in one smooth move, bringing her beneath him.

"Now," Marlow demanded and he drove into her with one stroke.

Oh, Lord. She was hot, wet, and just as tight as before. He pulled back, almost all the way out, and then slowly sank back into her wet clasp. Her inner muscles clung to him, pulling him even further into her grip.

"Liam," she said, as he slowly pulled himself back again, trying to make it last longer, "move faster." He would have laughed if he hadn't been in so much pain. He did speed up, but

just enough to drive both of them crazy. She encircled his waist
with her legs and shuddered as her thighs tightened on his hips.

He quickened his pace and her muscles tightened around
his shaft. Liam looked down just in time to see her eyes go
vague with complete abandon as her muscles convulsed around
him, pulling him further into her. Two more strokes and he
exploded, her name on his lips.

* * * *

The first streams of light slid across the room, giving Liam
a wonderful view of Marlow as she slept. For the first time, she
was completely relaxed. He propped himself up on his elbow,
and watched her even breathing. She lay on her stomach, the
pink sheet only coming to her waist. Her back was slender and
unmarred by so much as a freckle. He fingered her straight
spine, so delicate but strong.

Liam hardened when he thought of everything they had
done the night before. He had always considered himself a sensualist. In about every facet of his life, he reveled in sensuality.
From music to food to women, he loved to savor. But, last
night, Marlow took him to an almost hedonistic height of en-
joyment.

They savored each other's bodies, trying to satisfy their un-
fulfilled hunger. But with each touch, hand to breast, tongue to
nipple, nothing seem to quench it. He was thinking about pulling the sheet down and kissing her sweet ass when he heard his
cell phone ring.

Heath and his parents were the only ones who had the
number, so he jumped off the bed, trying to get to it before it
woke Marlow. He grabbed his jeans off the floor and heard
Marlow grumble.

"Liam, where the hell have you been?" his brother asked.

He sat back on the bed. "I'm in Abilene."

"Where are you in Abilene? You're not in your hotel room."

Marlow's hand glided up his back and he turned around. She was leaning back on the pillows, sheet still at her waist, her beautiful breasts streaked with the morning sun. Her eyes were only half opened and her lips curved into a sleepy, satiated smile.

"Have you been checking up on me, bro?"

"I just wanted to make sure you remembered Mom's birthday."

"Have I ever forgotten?"

"No, but you haven't been yourself lately."

"What do you mean?" he asked and frowned when Marlow's hand slipped away. He looked at her and saw concern in her eyes. Liam shook his head, telling her not to worry, but she didn't reach out to him again. Instead, she scooped up a blue robe off the chair next to the bed and put it on. She padded barefoot to the bathroom, probably wanting to give him a little privacy.

"I mean you've been a little strange for a few months. You haven't been dating as much, and if I didn't know better, I would say you were mooning over some woman. But I guess I was wrong. When I couldn't get a hold of you this morning, I got a little worried."

"Yeah." He didn't moon. Never. He didn't need to worry if some woman loved him or not. He was independent.

He glared at the door. *What the hell was taking so long in the bathroom? Marlow should've been out already.*

"Well, it's nice to know there are willing women anywhere you go, Liam. Just tell me it's not someone who's going to be mad when you dump her."

"No one ever gets mad at me. I've been invited to more weddings of ex-girlfriends than any guy I know."

"Abilene is a little different than Dallas, big brother. It's a little more conservative and women are a little more careful about things like that. Anyway, you just be careful. When are you heading up to Mom and Dad's?"

The door to the bathroom opened and Marlow stood there, a smile on her face. She had washed away all the sleep.

"Hmm? Oh, I'm leaving tomorrow night. I plan on getting in around midnight." Okay, so that was hours later than he had planned. But, with a little luck and a lot of charm, Liam could cuddle up to Marlow until nine on Sunday night.

She walked across the room, sat down next to him, and kissed his neck.

"You're only coming into town for one day? Well, she must be awfully good."

"What do you mean by that?"

"You usually spend the whole weekend up there. Mom is always telling me how much time you spend there, while I'm wasting away at work. I'm heading up today. For once, I'll be the good son, while you roll around in bed with one of your women."

Marlow stood and motioned she was going to make some coffee. He waited until she left the room to answer him.

"Marlow isn't like that, Heath. None of the women I see are like that."

There was nothing but silence for a few seconds. Then the usually unflappable Heath let loose a stream of profanity that amazed Liam.

"Marlow Smith? As in Hammond Smith's daughter?"

"Yeah."

"Lord, Liam, are you stupid? I talked to him and he seems like a nice guy, but from what I've heard, he's very protective of his daughter. This is the one thing you've never done. Neither one of us ever fools around with any woman who works for the company that hired us. But what do you do? You pick a woman who lives in a little city like Abilene and screw her. Not only that, you pick the boss's daughter."

"I don't need this, Heath. I don't need your judgmental crap this morning." He couldn't help getting defensive, especially because somewhere in the back of his brain, he knew Heath was right.

"I've poured my heart and soul into this company, Liam, and I'm not going to let you blow it because you couldn't keep your dick in your pants."

"Don't tell me about commitment to the company," he hissed. "You don't even want to go there. I know you're dedicated to this company, but the truth is, I am too. I work just as many hours as you, doing the things you don't want to do. You know, Heath, like go out and talk to humans. Interaction is not your forte — it's mine.

"And, although I know you give more time at the office, I work just as hard on the road. I spend more and more time away from Dallas because you don't want to do the one-on-one. So spare me the crap about how much you give to the company. I give just as much."

"I didn't mean—"

"No, you did mean it. To be perfectly honest, I'm sick and tired of everyone thinking I'm the airhead, out for only one thing."

Heath was silent for a few moments, then he said, "I'm

sorry, Liam. I know you give as much to this company as I do. It's just not like you to get involved with someone you're working with, that's all."

"I forgive you. I'm still mad at you, but I'll forgive you. Make sure you get a cake."

He hung up the phone, cutting off any remarks Heath might have made. Truth be told, Liam didn't understand why he had gotten so angry with Heath.

Heath and Liam were only two years apart in age. Growing up, their personalities had veered off into different directions. Friends, male and female, came easy to Liam. Heath studied. His dedication helped him graduate from college only a semester behind Liam. Both of them had graduated with honors, but Heath earned Liam's respect because he took an overload of classes, worked, and still graduated with honors.

They had been close enough to fight without getting too mad. But this argument rubbed Liam the wrong way. Why did he get so upset when Heath made comments about Marlow? Okay, so Mom would snatch Heath baldheaded if she had heard his comments, but usually, Liam would've laughed it off. He didn't feel so jovial at the moment, though.

The crack about keeping his dick in his pants had boiled his blood. *But, why?* He enjoyed women and never tried to hide it. Some people thought he enjoyed them too much. *So what?* Why had a comment Heath had made before, bother him today?

He took a deep breath, trying to calm his anger, when he caught movement out of the corner of his eye. Marlow stood, holding two cups of coffee, uneasiness evident in her eyes.

He smiled, feeling more of the anger drain from him. Just her presence seemed to calm him. At the same time, he grew heavy and heated at the sight of her in the powder blue robe.

Liam knew for a fact, there was nothing underneath that robe but smooth, ivory skin.

She walked forward, and he noticed the edge of her robe flapping open. He glimpsed a flash of ivory skin and he knew they were not going to have a long conversation over coffee.

* * * *

Marlow sensed the change in Liam immediately. The air between them thickened and warmth spread through her. With every fiber of her being, Marlow had fought this attraction. She had lain awake the night before, thinking of reasons why sleeping with Liam was wrong.

First, she thought she should be indignant she allowed Liam to weasel his way into her bed. Her muscles grew rigid with anger when she realized he had let her think she was in charge, giving her some kind of power trip. She was about to wake him up, when his hand slid across her stomach. The anger had disappeared and heat replaced it, rolling through her body.

Two hours later, the complications at work from this brief affair bombarded her. Work could become uncomfortable if they ended on a sour note. But she quickly ignored this argument because Liam would be gone soon.

Disappointment weighed her down with that one thought. She shouldn't care he would be leaving soon. In fact, she should be glad he was out of her vicinity. Before meeting him, she had been convinced she would never be sexually satisfied. She never understood what all the fuss was about. But now, all she had to do was think of those wonderful hands, or smell his cologne, and Marlow turned into a raging hormone. With him gone, she could go back to her life. Alone. All alone, the way she liked it. At least, the way she liked it before she walked up to him in a Dallas nightclub.

Panic, sharp and swift, burned in her belly and she knew, even if she kicked him out of her bed this morning, it was too late. She knew she would never be the same. Somewhere around three in the morning, she gave up. Even though she knew it would detrimental to her heart, she knew she would never be able to fight the attraction.

"Marlow," Liam said, his deep voice interrupting her thoughts, "are you okay?"

She walked to the bed, handed him his coffee and sat down beside him.

"Yes, I'm fine," she said. "Is everything okay? You never answered me."

He glanced at his cell phone on her nightstand and sighed. "Yeah, Heath and I just had an argument."

She placed her hand on his thigh and he looked away from the phone to her hand. Slowly, he raised his eyes, and a small, but totally wolfish, smile curved his lips.

She snatched her hand away and cleared her throat. Looking around the room, she desperately tried to find something more interesting to study than Liam. That was going to be hard because he was sitting in her bed, his hair disheveled from sleep, her sheet wrapped around his waist. Then, her eyes dipped to the sheet and his obvious arousal. Her breath caught in her throat and she had to swallow to cover it.

"You don't need to go, do you?" she asked.

"Naw," he said. She heard the laughter in his voice. "Heath and I argue all the time."

She looked up at him. "Must be hard to work together."

"No, we've been arguing since he could talk. Mom said she had us a little too close together." He lifted his hand and began to toy with the ends of her hair. "He was calling to remind me about Mom's birthday on Monday."

"Oh," she said because she didn't know what else to say. She also couldn't concentrate because he had moved his free hand to her thigh and was gently stroking the tender skin.

"Anyway, he made some comments I didn't appreciate. I should have just let it go but..." he said, shaking his head as if trying to clear his thoughts. He was looking at his hand on her thigh. The rise and fall of his chest increased in speed. "You have the most amazing skin. It's so soft and smooth. I'm afraid I'll hurt you." She didn't say anything, just watched his bent head.

"You seem so delicate." His finger inched up her thigh. "But you know what I think?"

He looked up when she didn't say anything. His green eyes were dark with passion.

"I think you're a lot tougher than you look. I think you're one tough lady. One sexy lady." She didn't say anything. She couldn't. Her heart thumped and accelerated to an unreasonable speed. Blood coursed through her body, pumping passion to every part of her being. She knew she was growing damp and the man had barely touched her.

"Marlow," his voice rough, and demanding, "I gotta have you, *now*."

Chapter 13

Liam stood. In the pale morning light, his erection jutted out from the coarse golden brown hair, hard and magnificent. He pulled her to her feet, grabbing her belt and yanking it open. Her robe fell open, but before he had time to look, he yanked it off her and threw it onto the floor.

His hands slid around her back, pulling her closer. His penis rubbed against her belly, hard and hot. She shifted and Liam groaned.

He bent his head but instead of kissing her face, his lips dipped down to her neck. A shock of energy seared through her when his teeth made contact with the sensitive skin. She could feel his coarse hair against her breasts and to ease the ache of her tight nipples, she rubbed against it. With that one move, Liam lost control. He bit her neck, not enough to hurt, just enough to send a rack of shivers through her.

"Get up on the bed, honey." She crawled up on the bed and began to lie down when he stopped her, positioning her on her hands and knees.

She heard her nightstand drawer open and close, and then the sound of foil ripping. A couple seconds later, the bed dipped from his weight as he positioned himself behind her.

He placed his hand on her stomach and leaned forward.

"I wish I could do this slower, but I just can't wait."

She mumbled something, she wasn't sure what. He rubbed his cock against the cleft of her bottom. She trembled as he stroked himself against her skin. Placing his knees between hers, he opened her even further. His hand moved down, caressing her folds. She knew she was wet and he shuddered at the discovery. He slid his palm to her stomach again and guided himself in with his other hand. The tip of his erection was at her entrance and then, without any warning, he entered her in one swift stroke.

Even though he prepared her, she winced at the invasion. He held himself still, stretching her to the limit. She could feel her inner walls pulse around his erection, but he still didn't move. Lightly, he continued stroking her.

Slowly, he pulled almost all the way out and then sank back into her. After a few strokes, she picked up his rhythm, slamming against him. Her fingers curled into the sheets on the bed as he slid in and out of her. His fingers caressed her clitoris as his rhythm increased. His hard abdomen slapped against her bottom. Every nerve in her body grew tighter, until she screamed in frustration. He increased the pressure of his fingers and all the pent up passion burst in a tidal wave of tremors.

"Oh yes, Marlow, baby. That's it, moan for me."

Liam shouted her name again, his body taut, his hand still pressing against her. He collapsed on top of her and she fell to the bed. He rolled over, pulling her next to him, wrapping his arm around her. His heat surrounded her, warming her. His hand glided up and down her arm and she shivered.

"Cold?" he asked and pulled the sheet up to cover both of

them. He kissed the top of her head and sighed. "I think you could be the death of me, woman. Where did you get all those condoms?"

She giggled, and then stopped herself because she never giggled.

"They were part of my birthday package from Joey."

He grunted. His arm tightened around her and he kissed her head again. She tangled her fingers in his chest hair, enjoying his warm skin, dewy with exertion. He smelled wonderful; musky from their lovemaking with just a hint of cologne. His muscles relaxed and his breathing slowed and evened and she knew he had fallen back to sleep.

She snuggled closer, reveling in the skin-to-skin contact, the closeness she felt. If she were smart, she would run as fast as she could away from him. He was dangerous because he made her feel things she had never felt before and because he had her wanting things with him she knew she could never have. She leaned up and kissed his chin and he smiled in his sleep. Somewhere along the way, she had fallen in love with him and there was no going back.

* * * *

Liam arrived at his parents' house sometime close to midnight on Sunday night. As he parked his Mustang behind Heath's SUV, he smiled, thinking about the reason he was so late. He had planned getting there sometime around suppertime, but he had waited until the last possible moment to leave. He just simply could not get enough of Marlow. He was an addict and the only drug to curb his hunger was Marlow and that sweet little body of hers.

What had started out as just a night of passion had quickly turned into a weekend filled with a bevy of sensual delights even he would be hard pressed to repeat. He had allowed her to take control, had been prepared to leave her Friday night, without touching her. He didn't believe in taking advantage of women who were emotionally wrung dry. But she wouldn't let him go, wouldn't allow him to leave her, and used that sweet mouth of hers on him. Shy, completely untutored, she had caused him to lose control.

He frowned at that thought. Normally, he didn't like losing control. Oh, he knew to truly enjoy sex, he had to lose a measure of his restraint. But, in the long run, he always managed to pace the sex, even the length of the relationship.

He grabbed his bag out of the passenger seat and got out of the car. On the way to the front porch, he paused because he had been rushing to call Marlow. Two hours and he was running to the phone like some lovesick idiot. He hadn't told her he would call but as soon as he got out of the car, he headed for the phone. He frowned even harder.

He enjoyed intimacy. He just didn't let it rule his life. Uneasiness knotted his stomach. Rubbing his free hand over it, he tried to ease the feeling.

As he walked up the front steps to the porch, he told himself he would not call her. Being a small town girl, she'd probably assume there was a serious relationship if he encouraged her with a phone call. He really didn't want that. Two more weeks would be enough for him. Well, it could take maybe three and definitely no more than four at the most.

No strings attached. That was what made him happy. That was the way things worked for him. He didn't need her for his well-being. He was a man who survived on his own, without a woman to tell him where he needed to be and when to be there. This comfort he derived from Marlow's presence was temporary. So what if he had slept more soundly in her bed than he had in the last three months?

He rubbed his hand over the knot in his stomach again. As he unlocked the front door, he couldn't shake the uneasy feeling he wasn't all that determined to finish up his work in Abilene.

* * * *

Wednesday morning, Marlow sat at her desk, looking over the plans she had drawn up for the Twelve Days of Christmas Campaign. When she had mentioned it to Liam last weekend, he had wanted to see her ideas on paper. She had spent the last two nights working on it. It had been the only thing that had helped her maintain her sanity the past two nights.

After Liam left Sunday night, a restless energy had consumed her. She just couldn't settle down. She would find something to distract her but memories of her weekend would sneak back into her mind, taunting her.

Part of her had hoped he would call. Marlow knew it was ridiculous to think she had occupied his thoughts at all while he was gone. Not the way he occupied hers.

Just one weekend spent with him, and she felt so alone when he left. That was definitely not a good sign. When Monday came and went and she didn't hear from him, she reassured herself it was what she wanted. Just a quick hot affair with no part of her heart involved. But when she found out he had called her father about something, a sharp stab of disappointment pierced her heart before she could stop it.

She dismissed the morbid thoughts and started working on the plan again. Joey knocked and then entered.

"Hey, boss woman, I got those figures you wanted on the

market research." She handed the papers to Marlow. "Have you heard from the stud?"

"Joey, I'd appreciate it if you would quit calling him that."

"Okay, has *Liam* called to check in with you?"

Marlow sighed. Joey had been dropping hints for two days trying to figure out what had happened Friday night.

"No, he talked to Dad yesterday." She studied the report but she could still feel Joey's eyes on her. Marlow looked up at her, pushed her glasses up her nose. "What?"

"He didn't call you after you spent the weekend in bed?"

"How'd you know about that?"

"I didn't, but you just confirmed what I was thinking."

She shot Joey a dirty look and returned to studying the report. "Liam doesn't need to call me. All we're having is a quick, little affair." Joey was silent for once and Marlow glanced up and met her suspicious stare. "He never said he was going to call. Stop looking at me like that. What we have is good sex, that's it." Joey shot her a disbelieving look, then turned around to walk out. Before she reached the door, she stopped and said, "Well, speak of the devil."

"Joey," Liam said, "my mother would kick your butt if she heard you call me that."

As he smiled at Joey, Liam couldn't believe how excited he was to reach Abilene. He would've been back the night before, but Heath had wanted to tag along and whined about driving in so late. He looked past Joey to see Marlow, dressed in one of her plain, boxy suits. Her hair was pulled back in a tight bun, her glasses perched on her nose and not a bit of makeup. The sight of her soothed and aroused him at the same time. She stood, looking a little uncertain, and then her eyes moved past him, resting on Heath.

He stepped aside. "Ladies, I would like you to meet Heath Campbell, my brother. Heath, this is Joey Vernon and Marlow Smith." He watched as Marlow's eyes widened at the sight of Heath.

Although he was eighteen months younger, Heath was six-foot-four, three inches taller than Liam. He was also bigger boned. Where Liam had golden brown hair and green eyes from their mother, Heath's chestnut brown hair and hazel eyes gave him the look of their father.

Instead of lying to him, Liam had told Heath the truth about his relationship with Marlow, swearing him to secrecy. He'd reassured Heath it was just a quick, little affair. Heath had made him swear he would wait until they finished their work with the company before he dumped her. Still worried Liam would blow the deal, Heath insisted on following him to Abilene.

"Well," Joey said, seductively. "It's so nice to meet you, finally."

Heath looked at her, quirked an eyebrow. "Finally?"

"We've been exchanging email the past few weeks."

"You're the executive assistant?" Joey bristled at Heath's disbelief. Both Heath and Joey were unattached, free to do what they wanted with each other, and Heath managed to piss her off in the first five minutes. Sometimes, he wondered if they were really related.

"Yes," she said, her voice sharper than Liam had ever heard it.

"Oh, you seemed so efficient."

"And I don't now?" Her teeth were clenched and her body bristled with anger.

"Joey," Marlow said. "Heath, I'm so glad to meet you." Liam met her eyes and winked. She dropped the paper she was holding. "Hmm, Liam didn't say anything about you accompanying him this week."

"I decided to stop in. I don't get to do this that often."

Yeah, Heath just wanted to make sure I didn't screw anything up.

"Oh, great." She picked up the paper she dropped and looked at Heath, giving him one of her real smiles. It brightened her face, bringing a sparkle to those big blue eyes. His breath caught in his throat. He just couldn't keep his eyes off her. She walked around the desk toward Heath, her lavender scent surrounding him as she walked by. He needed to figure out something for his brother to do. If he didn't get to touch her in the next ten minutes, he would go crazy.

"I have this report about the Twelve Days of Christmas promotion, profit-loss, stuff like that. I knew you handled this type of thing and I was going to fax it to you today. But, since you're here, we can go over it together."

"Hey, great idea." Great way to get rid of him so he could get his hands on Marlow. "Joey, why don't you show Heath where my office is? I've got a few things I need to discuss with Marlow."

Joey gave him a knowing look. She scowled at Heat. "Come on."

"Oh, how can I resist such a sweet invitation?"

"I assure you, there's nothing sweet about me."

She brushed past Heath and he followed her out the door, watching the sway of her hips. A small wolfish smile curved his lips. *So, Heath wasn't as put off by Joey as he pretended.* As soon as the door shut, he turned and realized Marlow had retreated behind her desk.

"How was your mother's birthday?" she asked.

Was there a hint of huskiness in her voice?

"Good." He walked around her desk, and took her hand in his, pulling her into his arms. She immediately melted her body to his. A surge of lust slowly rolled through his system. "How's work been?"

"Oh, okay. Daddy still thinks I'm wasting my time with the promotion idea."

He pulled her closer, pulling her in front of him. Her arms immediately went to his shoulders. He backed her up to the desk, bent his head, and started to nibble on her ear lobe.

"Liam, we can't do this."

He pulled away from her, thinking she meant to put a stop to any kind of physical contact. Anger sped through him.

"You can forget that, babe." His voice hard as granite.

"First of all, I told you to stop calling me babe. I think you do that so you don't have to remember names." That was one of the reasons he had started using it, but with Marlow, it was different. "Second of all, we could get caught in my office and I don't relish the fact of being fodder for the company gossip mill."

Relief quickly replaced the anger. He slid his hands around her waist, pulling her body flush with his once more. "And get that look out of your eyes, Liam. I mean it."

"But, Marlow, all I did was nibble on your ear. Just one little nibble." He bent his head and took the lobe in his mouth. "Don't tell me you were ready to jump my bones from just one little nibble?"

Taking her lobe between his teeth, he bit, then sucked. Her muscles relaxed and he pulled her closer. She had closed her eyes and he could feel her breasts rise and fall with each choppy breath. Oh, yeah, she was ready to jump his bones.

"Liam." She gave him a little push and he relented. "We have a lot to do today. We had a problem at one of the stores yesterday with that vendor and it was a mess. So I'm a day behind with my work and I was trying to catch up when you got here."

She reached across her desk and picked up a stack of file folders. As she flipped through them, he studied her, drinking in the sight. Never in his life had he rushed to a woman. They'd always chased him, so he was sure, at least in the beginning, the unrelenting need to posses her came from her refusal. Now, he wasn't so sure.

He'd spent his time at his folks' house, brooding about what she was doing in Abilene and getting strange looks from both his parents and Heath. Okay, maybe once or twice in elementary school he brooded about a girl, but he definitely never sat around thinking of the possibilities. He fought the urge to call all Monday and Tuesday. Late Tuesday afternoon, he had relented and called her father, asking about Marlow, just to make sure she was okay. This was getting a little pathetic.

He walked away from her and studied Abilene from her office window. Stuffing his hands in the pockets of his trousers, he tried to push away the unsettling emotions this woman evoked. Paper rustled behind him and it irritated him Marlow seemed unfazed by his presence. Frustration gnawed at his gut.

"Aren't you going to ask me why I didn't call?" His voice sharp was with anger. Really, shouldn't she be mad like every other woman?

She cleared her throat nervously. "Well, you didn't say you would call, Liam. I just assumed you would if you wanted to."

Anger rolled through him. He turned around to confront her and found her studying him with a wary eye.

"Maybe I did."

She sighed and placed the paper she had been studying on her desk.

"Then why didn't you call?"

"I don't know. And I didn't say I wanted to call, just *maybe* I wanted to call." He knew he sounded like a dork he just couldn't help it.

"Liam, I'm not a clingy type of woman. I know this relationship isn't going to outlast your stay in Abilene and I thought we both understood the rules. I didn't say I didn't want you to call. In fact, it would have been nice, but I figured you were spending time with your parents. I didn't think I ranked above your family." She sighed again. Then she looked him in the eye, a little smile curving her lips. "I did miss you."

That seductive smile and hint of huskiness in her voice sent heat to his groin. He pulled her into his arms, reveling in her soft, feminine curves. Excitement skittered through him. He bent his head again and nibbled on her neck, right at her pulse point. He smiled when it accelerated. He took a deep breath, reveling in her soft, feminine smell.

There was a sharp knock at the door and then it opened. Marlow immediately pushed him away, and turned around to see who it was.

Heath stood in the doorway, his hand on the doorknob, his mouth tightened into an angry line. He looked from Liam to Marlow and back to Liam. Liam had promised him he would cool it with Marlow, at least at the office.

Liam stepped up beside Marlow and looked at her from the corner of his eye. She was nervously trying to smooth back her hair and her face was fire engine red. She was so cute, how could he resist jumping her the moment he had the door shut? He slipped his arm around her waist, almost daring Heath to say something. When Heath remained silent, just narrowed his eyes, Liam decided to get the confrontation over with.

"What do you want, Heath?"

Chapter 14

"Joey said you have some market research on these." He completely ignored Liam and concentrated on Marlow, who seemed to have recovered.

"Yes," she said. "Let me get them for you." She tried to walk around him, but he wouldn't budge. After a little pushing she said, "Move it, Liam."

Heath was startled, judging by the look on his face. *Why not?* Liam knew Heath wasn't used to women ordering him around. Hell, Liam wasn't used to it.

Marlow rounded her desk, giving Heath one of her genuine smiles, and headed over to her file cabinet. Did she have to give every guy that smile? Liam glowered at Heath, who raised an eyebrow. *Shit!* Now his brother knew he was jealous of any man who received attention from Marlow. Heath glanced over at Marlow, and Liam did the same.

Marlow had bent at the waist, looking in the bottom drawer, the ugly tweed fabric of her suit stretched tight across her bottom. All intelligent thought flew out of his mind as he studied her cute little heart-shaped rear end. Now he knew what had made Heath smile. Then, as soon as he realized his brother was ogling his woman, he shot Heath a dirty look, which only made his smile widen. Liam fought the urge to jump over the desk and kick his brother's ass. Standing there, looking at Marlow. The nerve of him.

Liam crossed his arms over his chest and sent Heath another dirty look.

"Here you go, Heath," Marlow said.

"Thanks, I might need you to go over a few of these figures with me. Are you free for dinner tonight?" Heath asked.

"No, she's busy for dinner."

Heath coughed, suspiciously sounding like choked laughter.

"Liam, stop that." Marlow's face flushed an even brighter shade of red and he realized she was embarrassed, so he backed off, just a little. "Yes, I'm free for dinner, but I'd be happy to go over any questions you have at lunch."

Heath smiled at Marlow as he took the file folder from her. "Well, that's a date then." He sent Liam a smirk and headed out the door, closing it quietly when he left.

He glanced over at Marlow and found her with her hands on her hips, shooting blue daggers at him.

"Liam, you can't do that."

"Do what?"

"Answer for me."

"Why not?" He really couldn't understand himself. It never bothered him before if Heath admired one of his lovers.

"Because, you're no better than my father when you pull crap like that."

He softened just a bit. Marlow didn't want a man to run her life and she sure wasn't returning Heath's admiration. He reached across the desk, grabbed her arm, and slowly guided her around the desk and back into his arms. He nuzzled her neck, breathed in her scent, and relaxed just a little.

"Okay, I'll let you go, but we're having dinner tonight."

She nodded, without opening her eyes. Once he had her agreement, he released her.

"Oh, but what about Heath?"

"What about him? I'm not into sharing women. Let him get his own woman."

She laughed, one of those rare, completely free laughs, and his chest tightened.

"Liam, he just got into town and doesn't know anyone."

"He knows Joey."

She snorted. "There's no way she'll let him hang out with her now. If there's one thing that irritates Joey, it's when men think she's stupid because of her looks."

"Hey, he's a Campbell. You should know nothing gets us down." Because he just couldn't resist her lips, he bent down, gave her a hard, quick kiss that reached down in his gut, twisting that knot a little tighter. "Now, do you have a copy of the information you just gave Heath?" She nodded and he was satisfied to see the passion brimming in her eyes. "Well, let's get down to business then."

* * * *

Marlow sighed when she looked at the information included in the report to her father. Liam and his brother had agreed with her assessment. After several discussions, the three of them had decided that working up a proposal together and presenting it to her father would be their best bet. Heath knew her knowledge of the grocery business was far more reaching then either Liam's or his, so he wanted to include her in the proposal, which incorporated her Christmas promotion and the revamping of the older stores. Even though she knew the only way to get her father to listen to her ideas was to have a man back them, it still irritated her.

Marlow thought about the quiet brother, Heath. *You couldn't find two brothers so different from each other.* Both of them were handsome, although she was convinced Liam was better looking. However, where Liam was outgoing and flirtatious, Heath was quiet and serious. Taller than Liam by a few inches, he was bigger through the chest, built more like a linebacker. His coloring was also a little darker and his solemn eyes were the shade of chocolate. She could tell his job was important to him. He studied everything she had given him, took the time to consider the options, and gave her his observations. It would have been a pleasant working experience, if only Liam wouldn't have spent all his time trying to wedge between the two of them. He almost acted jealous of any time she spent with his brother. She shook her head at the ridiculous thought.

They had spent most of Friday morning going over her ideas, all of which he apparently admired. But every now and then, he seemed to study her like she was some kind of science experiment. Sitting in her office that morning, she'd glanced up to find his serious brown eyes fixed on her again. Not in the same sensual fixation Liam usually had, but as if he was trying to fit her into some kind of equation or puzzle. After quietly studying her for a few moments, he broke his silence and told her he was heading off to talk to Liam.

There seemed to be some kind of undercurrent between the two brothers and it had something to do with her. She couldn't put her finger on it, but every now and then, there would be a look between them that held some kind of meaning she couldn't figure out.

While Heath had gone back to the hotel last night, Liam, being who he was, assumed he would be staying with her from now on. She felt Heath wasn't really thrilled with the idea, she just didn't know why. The truth was, she really didn't care what he thought. And she was helpless to say no to Liam. He'd turned her into some kind of sex maniac. Knowing their time was limited, she didn't argue. She would grab what she could while he was there and then go back to the same old boring life she had before Liam.

As if conjured up by her thoughts, Liam walked through the door. The same secret smile he usually wore around her in place. Every nerve in her body jingled with anticipation. Her heartbeat tripped up and she was positive he knew, because his smile widened.

"Marlow, I thought we might take Heath to lunch today. He's decided to head out this afternoon and wanted to go over a couple things with you. And," he said, leaning up against her desk, "I thought we might do a little work after he left."

He had positioned his body next to hers and she could smell the outdoors mixed with soap and his cologne. Heat radiated off him, reaching out to her. She fought the urge to lean against him and enjoy the warmth.

"And what kind of work were you thinking about, Liam?" Her voice had dropped an octave.

He dragged his finger along her jaw line, then under her chin. His thumb brushed over her bottom lip.

"I had a figure or two I wanted to review and I thought you might be able to help."

She thought about the work she wanted to do this afternoon and the meeting she had with Ken. He must have sensed her hesitation because his fingers glided down her neck to the collar of her blouse. With a couple of quick flicks, he revealed her cleavage. His fingers dipped between her breasts. She shivered as a rash of goose bumps spread across her chest.

"I have a meeting with Ken this afternoon." Anger, not passion heated his eyes. But as fast as it appeared, it vanished. She must have been mistaken. Liam wouldn't get mad just because she would be spending time with Ken. That would mean he was jealous and possessive and those were two things she knew he was not. "Hmm," was all he said. His fingers traced over the lacy edge of her bra and her nipples tightened painfully. Electricity radiated from her breasts to the rest of her body, warming it from the inside out.

"I...I guess I could reschedule my meeting with him."

Liam didn't say anything. His eyes never left hers as his fingers found the front closure of her bra and popped it open. Her surprised gasp filled the room. His head bent and his breath warmed her nipple a moment before his tongue slid across it.

"Liam," she admonished as she backed away from him. "What the heck are you thinking?"

He shrugged. "I locked the door." The truth was, he didn't know what had come over him. Every time she mentioned Moore, an overwhelming need to stake his claim on her almost choked him. He watched as she fastened her bra and buttoned up her blouse.

The past couple of days had been hard on him. He worked with her all day, but she insisted they keep it professional at the office. Meaning he had to keep his hands off her. He respected her decision and understood why she wanted it that way. Hell, if he was professionally involved with a woman, he usually insisted they keep it that way.

With this woman, keeping his hands off her in the office was driving him damn near insane by the end of the day. The past two nights had been incredible, rushing from the office and making love all night.

Waking her up in the morning had been one of the best things he had done in his life. Marlow never jerked awake, ready to start the day. She awoke slowly, grumbling the whole time. This morning, he had surprised her by sliding down in between her legs, giving her a good morning kiss she would never forget. This strange mixture of possession and lust confused him and had him doing things he normally wouldn't do.

He cleared his throat suddenly embarrassed by the way he was acting. Maybe rushing back to Abilene hadn't been such a good idea. Apparently, the time and distance hadn't been enough to bring any semblance of sanity to the overwhelming lust she inspired in him.

She looked at her watch. "We better get going. You know how the places fill up for lunch around here."

"Yeah." He took a deep breath and thought about bailing, maybe even running back to Dallas for the weekend, but then he looked at her blue eyes and her smile, and knew there was no way he would give up any time he had left with her. "I thought maybe we could hit Betty Rose."

"Then we better hurry. They don't have a lot of seating."

He nodded and followed her out the door, wondering just what he was going to do when it came time to leave.

* * * *

Marlow and Liam spent the next week creating a plan for revitalizing the small market stores. Throughout all of their discussions and all of their arguments, she had sensed he genuinely admired her business sense. He wouldn't always agree with her, but he listened to her arguments.

That Sunday night, they were working in her home office. She had set up the extra bedroom in her apartment as an office because she didn't like staying late by herself. When everyone left at the end of the day, she would jump at every little sound.

It had been over a week since Heath had left and she couldn't get anything out of Liam about their disagreement. She sighed and he looked up from what he was studying and smiled at her. He returned to the market report Heath had sent him. She knew that if he wouldn't even tell her about an argument he had with his brother — apparently over her — then they really didn't have anything. She suppressed another sigh and set her mind to her work. They were presenting their report to her father tomorrow morning.

After five minutes, she gave up. She just couldn't concentrate with Liam sitting on the floor beside her, wearing nothing but a pair of black silk boxers. Her blood warmed as she studied him while he worked. His golden brown hair, his green eyes, hell, even his chest hair turned her on. He had turned her into a raging hormone.

They'd been working for several hours, but anytime her mind wandered to him, she lost track of what she was doing. Especially when he shifted just right, and she could see the outline of his sex. All she could think about was walking over to him and jumping his bones. It didn't help that each time she shifted to ease her ache she was reminded that she was only wearing one of his dress shirts.

She groaned in frustration and Liam shot her a confused look. Deciding she didn't feel like waiting for him to make a move, she deliberately set down the paper she had been reading and crawled over to him.

"Something wrong?" She shook her head and removed her glasses, placing them on the desk. "You sound like you're frustrated with the work." She shook her head again. Sitting back on her heels, she unbuttoned the dress shirt. His eyes darkened and his breathing sped up.

She reached the last button and took off the shirt, all the while watching his face for reaction. Naked as the day she was born, she leaned over, took the book he held and set it on the ground.

"I'm sick of reports, Liam." She took a deep breath as she straddled him. The material of his shorts felt cool against her skin, the long ridge of his penis nestled between her legs. Gyrating her hips just a bit, she elicited a groan from both of them. She wrapped her arms around his neck and continued moving her hips while she bent down to kiss him.

She nibbled on his lower lip, sucking and nibbling, growing damper each time he groaned in appreciation. His cock thickened and grew, pressing against her. Tension gathered in her belly and slid down, pulsing between her legs. He groaned again, but this time it was filled with a hint of another kind of passion, something almost out of control. Pleased she could do this to him, she continued teasing him until he took her face in his hands and kissed her so hard, she felt it down to her toes.

Bolts of electricity shot through her, heating her blood. His hands moved to her back, and before she knew his intentions, he rolled her over, stretching out on top of her. He kissed her again, wet and deep, tangling his tongue with hers. He broke away for a moment, and she moaned in protest until she realized he was going for a condom.

Within moments, he was entering her, filling her. God, he was so long and so hard, she felt stretched to the limit, but she didn't care. She could feel her muscles pulsing around him, pulling him. As he pumped into her, she met him stroke for stroke, biting and clawing him.

She was desperate. Marlow knew she couldn't wait much longer. Liam shifted, bringing himself to his knees as he held onto her hips. He stroked deeper. The tension tightened painfully.

"Come, Marlow, baby, come for me. I want to see you come," he said, pumping into her, pushing her to her limit. "Yeah, that's it!" His hands gripped her hips tightly as he stroked and pushed.

"Oh, baby, that's it! That's it!" Liam said.

A few more strokes, and he shouted her name as he slammed into her one more time. She opened her eyes to watch his muscles tense, her name on his lips again. He was so male, so wonderful, and so beautiful. Watching him sent heat spiraling, shattering her as convulsions raced through her. Her mind was wiped clean, raw from the emotions churning inside her. She couldn't think of anything but him. Nothing was left but the one emotion pulsing through her.

"I love you, Liam."

Chapter 15

"So, you ready to come back to Dallas for awhile?" Heath asked.

Liam turned away from the window in the conference room to look at his brother. Since their last discussion about Marlow, they hadn't broached the subject. And, although he didn't mention her by name, he knew exactly what Heath was referring to.

"Yeah, sort of feel like I haven't been home for a year." He smiled but he knew it was a weak effort.

"Um…Liam, you've been a little distracted for the last couple days. I was wondering…well…are you okay?"

"Yeah."

But he wasn't. He realized something yesterday. This whole time, he had been kidding himself, trying to convince himself this obsession with Marlow, this unquenchable lust that ruled his life, was temporary. He supported her business ideas without question. They were great ideas but that wasn't the reason he had backed them.

His need for this presentation to succeed was tied up in his need for one little woman. Not the type of need he was used to fulfilling. Not a need that would be solved with heavy breathing and silk sheets. This need to see her happy, to support her through everything, no matter how bad it was, ruled his life. He didn't want to see her hurt because if she hurt, he hurt too.

He understood one thing: he was in love with her. This wasn't a need for sex, a blazing passion that would fizzle out in a few months. This was knee-deep, knock-you-on-your-ass, punch- drunk love and he didn't know what to do about it. When she had shouted out she loved him last night, he had held her, kissed her and then carried her to her bedroom and made slow love to her. He knew then he returned her feelings, but they were too new and too scary for him to discuss, even with Marlow.

"I'm fine, stop worrying. I'm the older brother here." He was closer to Heath than he was to anyone else in the world but he couldn't talk to him about his feelings for Marlow. Hell, just thinking about it knocked him to his knees. "I'll be back in Dallas and off to the next assignment before you know it."

Heath let go of a breath and said, "Thank God. I was worried you were hung up on her or something. She's definitely not your usual type. You're better off just letting go and moving on. All kinds of problems with a woman like her. Just send her a note once we get back to Dallas, after the check clears."

Liam didn't respond. There was no way he could tell Heath he wasn't sure he could live without Marlow.

* * * *

Marlow paused outside the conference room. Liam and Heath were inside, their tone serious and hushed. Thinking they needed privacy, she waited. Then Heath's voice rose slightly.

"All kinds of problems with a woman like her. Just send her a note once we get back to Dallas, after the check clears."

She waited for Liam to deny Heath. Tell him what they had been more than work and good sex. But silence seeped from the room.

Fearing they would come out of the conference room and find her in the hall, she hurried to her office, thankful Joey wasn't at her desk. She shut her door, leaned up against it, and then slid down to the ground.

Numbness filled her first. She just didn't feel anything at all. She played the words over in her head, trying to make something good out of them.

Pain so hot and fast seared her heart. He had just been making time with her and wanted to make sure he got out of town before he dumped her. Hell, he wanted to make sure the check from her father cleared before he broke it off. Tears welled up in her eyes as she thought of how he must be laughing at her confession last night. Telling him she loved him, the lothario of Dallas.

She choked back a sob as she thought of what a fool she had made of herself. Why would Liam, a man who had his pick of women, want her? No reason, except to make his stay here interesting and make sure he got paid well.

She angrily dashed away a tear that had rolled down her cheek. Well, she wouldn't let him have the upper hand. She would walk into that meeting, her head held high, and let him know she was a professional.

Then she would dump him. She wouldn't wait around for him to dash off a note; she would do the dumping. Then she would crawl in her bed for a week and cry.

* * * *

He was so in tune with her, he could feel her every emotion. Right now, she was skidding along a thin sheet of nerves and he was afraid she would break. They'd made their presentation to her father and the board members and were waiting for the board's response.

He didn't know how he was going to do it, but somehow, they would be together. He really didn't want to know what he would do if they weren't. A totally unfamiliar feeling swept over him and he realized that he was nervous about the outcome of his discussion with Marlow. Nothing had ever been so important to him.

The door to the conference room opened and Moore called them in. He followed Marlow through the door and the board looked like they were ready to send someone to death row. He knew Ham had convinced them they didn't need to follow Marlow's part of the plan.

All older men, most of them in their fifties and sixties, sat behind a huge mahogany table. Ham sat in the middle, with three of them on each side, Moore sitting off to the side.

"Campbell, I agree with a lot of the ideas you've presented today. I agree, money is needed for these smaller stores, but," Hammond paused for a second, flicking a look of concern at his daughter, "we're not going to go with that. We're going to go with your plan for expansion, slowing down just a bit, not using credit. But, I really don't want to sink any money into the older stores."

He glanced at Marlow. Other than being slightly pale, she showed no emotion whatsoever. Liam knew how important this had been to her and was puzzled by her reaction.

Within minutes, they were in her office and he was pulling her into his arms. She didn't melt against him like she usually did.

"I'm sorry, baby. I thought for sure that your father would at least go for the promotion idea." He stroked her back and panic churned in his stomach. She was acting aloof and rigid, so like the woman he met when he had arrived in Abilene a few weeks ago.

Marlow pulled away from him. She had to. Allowing him to hold her, comfort her, was dangerous. She had to make a break and make it quickly or she would lose her nerve.

She looked at him. Oh God, he was so beautiful it almost hurt to look at him. For the first time in a long time, she thought about a life outside of work, having a companion to talk to at night, someone to share things with.

No, she had to do this.

"Well, I guess you and Heath will be heading out tonight." She walked around the desk to put some distance between them. If she didn't, she would jump back into his arms and beg him to stay. "You packed all your things this morning, didn't you?"

His eyes showed confusion, but he shook his head. "Yeah, although I was thinking about staying for a few more days."

Her pulse leapt at the idea. Liam with her for a few more days. A few more hours of love making, of laughing together.

No! She had to be strong.

"Oh, I just figured you'd leave today."

A flash of pain crossed his face but she stamped down on the tender feelings welling up. This had to be done.

"Well, I just thought after last night…what you said and all…"

Oh he was trying to make her hurt.

"Oh, that. You know, Liam, it's just sex talk. Heat of passion, that sort of thing," she said, trying to keep her voice a bit on the cold side.

The pain she saw in his eyes seemed to intensify but she knew she had to be mistaken. He planned on dumping her once he left, so why would he be hurt?

"We said it was just while you were in town, Liam. You know, just a little fun on the side." With each word, pain seared through her, slicing her heart.

The look of pain changed, anger swiftly replacing it. She'd been right. He wasn't hurt by her rejection of his offer. He was angry he was being dumped, nothing else.

"Well then, I guess this is where I say it's been fun." His voice dripped with sarcasm. "Let me know if you or any of your friends are in need of my services."

He turned away, walked to the door, and opened it with a jerk. Heath and Joey were scowling at each other, but Liam never said a word. He walked past both of them and Heath followed. Marlow stood there, holding onto her dignity, refusing to cry, while she watched him walk out of her life.

Joey, concern in her eyes, stepped into her office and closed the door.

"What happened?" Joey asked.

All the pain, everything she had held back, bubbled to the surface and a sob escaped before she could stop it. Joey rushed over and embraced her.

"Oh, sweetie, did he dump you?"

Between sobs, she told Joey everything: hearing what went on this morning, what she had said to Liam last night. After fifteen minutes, her nose stuffy and her tear ducts dried out for the moment, she pulled away from Joey.

"I'm so sorry, hon, this is all my fault."

"No," Marlow said, looking out the window. "No, I fell in love with him when I knew he wouldn't be able to commit." The pain still rolled in her stomach. "The only thing left to do now is burn my sheets, eat some chocolate, and get on with my life."

* * * *

Liam stormed through the parking lot, trying to control his anger. *But maybe he shouldn't.* If he didn't allow the anger to boil his blood, he knew the pain would unman him.

He sensed Heath following him and continued to his car. The cold north wind nipped at his face, almost numbing it. He reached his car, standing beside it, not knowing what to do next.

"Liam," Heath said, placing his hand on Liam's shoulder, "what's going on? You didn't break it off with her, did you? I told you to wait until we got back to Dallas."

Liam laughed without humor. "Well, see, she's got you there, bro. She dumped me."

Just saying the words hurt. He'd been ready to settle down, marry her, have a ton of kids. The thought of Marlow, big with his child, sent hurt spiraling through him. For the first time in his life, he'd wanted to be the one who got the girl. But she'd rejected the idea. Hell, she hadn't even let him tell her how he felt.

"Well, that was easy. At least we don't have to worry about her father pitching a fit just because you fooled around with his daughter."

Liam grunted but still didn't turn around. The idea of spending his life without Marlow was unthinkable. How was he supposed to get the woman out of his blood? How? He loved her. He loved the fact she straightened every picture she walked by. He loved her strange sense of humor and her passion for neatness. Hell, he even loved those God-awful suits she wore.

He wasn't ready to face the idea of life without her, but Marlow didn't give him a choice. She had pushed him aside, telling him she didn't love him. *Oh, that hurt the most.*

He had spent most of the night before just watching her sleep. Moonlight dappling her skin, her cute little snore, he reveled in the idea he would get to do that for the rest of his life.

Then he had walked into her office and she had sliced his heart to shreds.

Heath cleared his throat and Liam realized it was freaking cold. He swallowed the pain and turned around. Heath studied him, trying to decipher his mood. Liam couldn't tell him anything. Revealing his hurt, this searing pain, would make it all too real.

"I'm going to take a few days off and go see mom and dad."

Heath raised his eyebrows but didn't conflict him. "Okay. You have a couple of weeks before you need to head down to Houston to work with that factory. You know, Candance called the office a couple times while you were out of town."

Candance Walker, Houston Rockets cheerleader, one of the best bodies he had ever touched. Not one spurt of interest.

"Yeah, well, maybe I'll look her up. Call me if you need anything."

He got in his car and drove away, knowing with each passing mile, he was further way from the woman he loved, the woman he needed to make his life whole. He just didn't know if he would ever be able to put it behind him and go on. Liam knew he needed to brood and he went to the one place on Earth where he could do that.

Chapter 16

Marlow sat at her dining room table, sipping coffee and thinking about Liam. For the past four days, she did little else but think about the jerk.

Why did she always seem to fall for the wrong guy? Why couldn't someone like Ken do it for her? She thought, at some point, some kind of a spark would ignite between the two of them, but nothing had happened. Well, if Liam hadn't came into town, she might've been able to get something going with Ken, but, to be honest, she knew Ken could never compete with Liam.

Liam. Even thinking his name hurt. When Vic had rejected her three years ago, she thought she had been devastated. These past few days, she realized she'd been embarrassed. Because, when you got right down to it, she'd never really loved Vic.

But now, she knew without a doubt she loved Liam. It had all started out so simple. No strings attached. But, somewhere along the line, she started wanting those strings attached. She wanted to come home to Liam at the end of the day. For the first time in years, she thought about having children. And she wanted to have them with Liam. He'd only wanted a quick affair to keep him going in Abilene. Something or someone to

187

keep him from getting bored.

Banging on her door interrupted her thoughts. She glanced at the clock on the wall and wondered who would be coming to her apartment at eight on a Sunday morning. Her coffee cup in hand, she walked to her door, opened it and found Ben standing on her doorstep, an angry expression clouding his face. Whiskers littered his jaw, his shirt was inside out, and he was clutching a paper in his hand.

"I'm sorry, Marlow. I tried to stop him. I told him to call."

Marlow looked over Ben's shoulder to see Janice, with an apologetic look on her face.

"Ben, let Janice come in and sit down. What are you thinking, dragging her out this morning? She needs her rest." She pushed Ben aside and took Janice's arm, guiding her to the couch. After making sure Janice was comfortable, she turned to find a very angry Ben, glowering at her.

"What the hell is the matter with you?" she asked.

"This!" He shoved the crinkled newspaper at her. "You told me you were going to tell your father to take a hike. You can't go through with this."

She took it and realized it was the lifestyle section of the Sunday paper. She studied it, confused, until she saw the announcement.

Moore-Smith

Hammond and Clarice Smith announce the engagement of their daughter, Marlow Jane Smith, to Kenneth Edmond Moore. The wedding will take place June 19.

At first, disbelief at what her father had done stunned her. Never in her life would she have guessed he would take this step. In fact, she wasn't even aware her father had hired Ken as a potential husband for her. Then fury boiled in her. She couldn't believe her father had done this to her. She had lived with her father's condescending attitude about her opinions, accepted the fact he would never take her seriously. This is how he repaid her. Marriage to a man who did nothing more for her than watching Lawrence Welk.

"From the look on your face, I take it you didn't know," Ben said.

She looked at him and realized he was no longer directing anger in her direction.

"Of course I didn't know anything about this. Jeez, I can't believe—"

Another round of banging interrupted her. *What was this? Grand Central Station?* She stalked over to the door, wrenched it open, and found Joey, her hair in a ponytail and wearing sweats, a furious expression on her face.

"Come on in and join the crowd. I have a feeling you read the paper."

"Ben, Janice," Joey said. "So, who's at fault? Your father or Ken?"

"I'm really not sure." Marlow rubbed her forehead. "My father probably instigated it."

"What are you going to do?" Janice asked.

Marlow glanced around the room at the varying expressions. Ben was furious, as was Joey, but Janice shot her a sympathetic look.

"I'll tell you one thing, I'm *not* marrying Ken." She mulled over everything that happened in the last three weeks. "And, I'm going to have a little chat with my father."

* * * *

Marlow parked her car in her parent's driveway beside Ken's SUV. Well, even if it had started out as her father's idea, Ken was now on board.

"Are we going to sit out here all morning?" Marlow glanced over at Joey.

When she decided to confront her father, Ben had wanted to come with her. Janice and Joey helped her convince him it wouldn't be a good idea. Joey said she would come for emotional support and there was no budging her. She even refused to change into something different, wearing the same Texas Tech sweat suit. Joey thought she looked a mess but Marlow thought she looked like a college boy's wet dream come true.

"No, but I confirmed a few things." Joey looked past her at the SUV. Fear welled up inside her, making her second-guess her fast trip over there. She wasn't really sure if she was ready to confront her father, but the truth was, he hadn't left her a choice. "Well, it's now or never."

She got out of the car and headed for the front door. She heard Joey slam the car door and follow her up the pathway to the house.

Using her key, she unlocked the front door. She headed to the kitchen and found her mother pouring a cup of coffee for Ken, her father sitting at the table with a smug look on his face.

"Marlow, my girl. I take it you saw the paper today?"

"Marlow," her mother said, setting the coffee pot down and rushing forward to hug her. "I'm so happy for you and Ken. When your father told me you were engaged, I was thrilled. He's such a good young man, and from such a good family. Why, we have to start planning. We have less than nine months to plan and so much to do."

Marlow looked at Ken to see his reaction and saw the same

smug smile her father sported. She shifted her attention back to her father.

"Mummy, I hate to disappoint you, but I'm not getting married."

"What? What are you talking about, Marlow? Ham, what is she talking about?"

"Now, Marlow——"

"Don't you now Marlow me! I'm not going to marry Ken. I don't love him." She heard her mother gasp but she studied her father. Her announcement had first turned his face red, then purple.

"I'm not going to be forced into another marriage I don't want. I've been down that road before and I really don't want to be there again."

"Marlow, honey, you need to calm down. I don't understand what's going on here." She looked at her mother, relieved to see confusion in her eyes. Well, at least her mother wasn't in on the scam.

"Mummy, daddy picked Ken for my next husband. For some reason, he seems to think I need to be married. So, because we weren't clicking, he decided to speed things up. He made the announcement. I'm sorry, mummy, but I refuse to marry Ken."

Her mother's eyes widened and then narrowed when she turned them on her father.

"Hammond," she said in the shrill voice that meant you were in big trouble, "is what Marlow said true?"

"Now, Clarice, Marlow just didn't move fast enough."

"Hammond Michael Smith, just what is going through your head?" Her mother's English accent sharpened.

Her father looked scared. *Well, who wouldn't be?* Her

mother was really terrifying when she was mad. But she refused to sympathize with him.

"I told you, our daughter is fully capable of making up her own mind."

"Clarice—"

"You know, if I let you run over me the way Marlow has allowed it all these years, I'd have gone insane. Do you think for one moment I raised a stupid girl?"

Her father, being a survivalist, shook his head.

"Marlow, I think we should talk." Ken was looking at her with understanding.

"Ken, I like you, you're a really nice guy, but I don't love you."

"That's alright," he smiled, "I admire you but I don't love you, either."

"But you're willing to marry me?"

"Yes. I'm not looking for a great passion, Marlow. I'm looking for a companion."

"Well, I don't want a companion. If I wanted a companion, I'd get a dog."

"Marlow, you shouldn't let what went on with Campbell color your decision."

"First of all, my relationship with Liam is none of your business. Second of all, you and my father have taken the decision away from me."

"You heard your father. We would never make any progress if we waited on you."

Her parents and Joey were paying attention to every word. Their sick fascination reminded her of rubberneckers at a car wreck.

"I'm not marrying you, Ken."

"Marlow, think about it." He walked past her father and stopped in front of her. "We get married, I run the company, and you can settle down."

"Settle down?" Her voice strained from the effort to strangle the scream gathering in her throat.

"Yes. You'll settle down and become a wife and mother."

"Wife and mother," she said, her voice a hoarse whisper. Anger simmered in her belly. It surged, rising up and boiling over. "What makes you think that's all I want out of life? To be *your* wife?"

Ken's eyes blazed. He held his anger under his cool veneer, but it lashed out at her.

"What are you waiting for? It's not like Campbell is going to marry you. He was using you."

"What's this about Campbell?" her father asked, but she ignored him.

Pain sliced through her. It was nothing new she'd dealt with it the past four days. It must have shown on her face because Ken's lips curled into a sneering smile.

"He slept with you and then dumped you."

She winced at the expletives streaming out of her father's mouth.

"Yes, we were sleeping together, however, the parting was mutual, and I never expected marriage." At least that much was true. She wanted it, but never expected it. "If I wasn't going to marry you before, I'm definitely not marrying you now."

"Well, if I would've known you were such a little slut, I would have taken you to bed. Maybe you wouldn't be walking around like an idiot, moping over a guy who's probably laughing at how naïve you are."

"Really, and just what makes you think I would sleep with

you? What makes you think you're good enough to sleep with me?"

He grabbed hold of her arm and yanked her to the side, out of earshot of their audience.

"You think some little nobody from Abilene is more important than I am? Your family is one generation away from white trash, Marlow. You should have been begging me to take you to bed." His eyes had taken on an evil light. The grip he had on her arm threatened to leave bruises as he was digging his fingers into her arm. Fear curled into her belly, souring the contents. She swallowed past the bile and jerked her arm away from him.

She refused to allow him to intimidate her. Fear transformed into fury. She was sick of being the one who stayed in control. The one who smiled when her father hired jackasses like Ken to run the company. The one who accepted her father's condescending attitude. She studied Ken, his evil sneer, and his holier than thou attitude.

Before she could stop herself, she curled her fist and punched him right in the nose. The crunch of bone turned her stomach. He screamed like a little girl. His hands immediately went to his nose, trying to stem the flow of blood.

She looked at her father to find him staring at her as if he didn't recognize her. Ken continued to shriek.

"If you hired him hoping for a son-in-law, I'm sorry. If you hired him thinking he could run the company, you're up a creek. You should have picked me for the job." She dragged in a deep breath and then did something she thought she would never do. "I love you, daddy. I quit."

She turned and walked out of the kitchen, leaving her father sputtering. Joey hurried after her.

"It's about time," Joey said as they both headed to her car.

"Yeah, well I quit and I lost your job in the process."

"That's okay. We'll figure out what to do."

When they were driving down Rebecca Lane, Joey said, "We could start our own business. With your knowledge and my organization, we could do it."

Marlow mulled over the suggestion. Running her own business. Being her own boss. She glanced at Joey and saw serious commitment in her eyes.

"Yes. I like that idea." She turned into their apartment complex. "Maybe we should start a grocery store. Run Smith's out of business."

Joey snorted. "I was thinking along the lines of an escort service."

A bubble of laughter burst out of Marlow. "Well, we'd have to move. Abilene would never go for that."

She parked her car in her designated spot. Joey joined her in a cup of coffee once they got into her apartment.

"We could do consulting," Joey said. "We could move to Dallas, start our own consulting firm."

Tears gathered in Marlow's eyes before she could stop them. One rolled down her cheek and she angrily swiped it away. All the pain — Liam leaving, her father's betrayal — gathered in her throat.

"Oh, honey." Joey got up and pulled Marlow into her arms. Sobs racked her body as all the pain pulsed through her. "I'm so sorry. I shouldn't have suggested that. You go ahead and cry. You deserve it."

She continued to cry, letting all the hurt break free. She cried for the pain of never being the daughter her father wanted and she cried for the pain of losing Liam. Finally, when she was cried out, Joey pulled back from her.

"Feel better." Marlow sniffled and nodded. "Good." Joey guided her over to the couch. "Now, don't worry about anything. We'll figure it all out." She sat down beside Marlow, swung her arm over her shoulders. "We are women, we are strong."

Marlow gave a watery chuckle. "Yeah, well, my hand hurts. Who would have known he could squeal like a little girl?"

They dissolved into giggles.

* * * *

About seven that night, her doorbell rang. Well, at least it was different from the banging of the morning. She stood on her tiptoes, looked through the peephole, and saw her father. Surprised, she opened the door.

"Daddy," she said warmly.

"Can I come in?"

"Sure." She stepped aside and let him pass.

"Nice place," he said, studying her living room. She realized in the two years she had lived here, her father had never visited. Her mother had been there many times, but her father had never once stopped by.

"Thanks."

The uncomfortable silence stretched.

"Do you want something to drink?"

"No." He was silent for a moment, as if unsure of what to say. "I didn't know if you would let me come in." He swallowed nervously.

"Not let you come in? I'm mad at you, but I would never do that."

"I'm really sorry about everything. I shouldn't try to run your life."

"I know you do it out of love. But, to be honest with you, it's partially my fault." When he looked like he wanted to argue, she stopped him. "I should've said something sooner."

"Well, your mother gave me hell when you left. After she kicked Ken out of the house."

She chuckled. "I would have liked to have seen that."

"It wasn't pretty. He was still shrieking like a little girl and screaming that we were going to pay to clean his shirt." He hesitated for a moment. "Are you sure you forgive me?"

She had never seen her father so unsure of himself. "Of course. I'm still irritated, but you're my daddy." His whole body seemed to relax and he opened his arms. She practically jumped at him and he gathered her into a hug. "Did he stop crying?"

He laughed. "You broke his nose." He pulled her to his side and his tone sobered. "I had no idea there was anything going on between you and Campbell."

"There was. But it's over. I knew when I started the affair, he wasn't going to settle down."

"If you want me to, I can hurt him." She knew he could. Not so much physically, but monetarily. One word from him could probably do serious damage to Campbell and Associates.

"No, Daddy. I could never let you do that. You see I love him. Nothing will come of it, but I'm like you. I protect the ones I love. I would have to hurt you if you did anything to him."

"Well, the boy better not show his face in Abilene. After your mother took care of Ken, she wanted to go after Campbell. You sure he doesn't want to marry?"

"Daddy, you know what kind of man Liam is. He's not into settling down." She pulled away from him, but still held his hands in hers.

"Well, maybe—"

"No, daddy, it's best I face the truth. I knew it when I started the affair and I was the one who ended it. Why would I want a man who didn't want me? Who didn't want the things out of life I wanted? No," she released his hands, "no, it's better this way. I'll find someone to have those babies with, I promise."

* * * *

Days after leaving Abilene, Liam was still at his parent's house in Henrietta. He spent most of his time helping his father with the chores, working in the garden and what not. The rest of the time, he spent thinking about Marlow and all that had gone wrong in such a short time.

"You know I love you, Liam," his mother said and he turned to watch her walk from the doorway with a glass of ice tea in her hand.

She gave him the tea and sat down beside him. Maggie Campbell was not a big woman. She was about average height, with curly gray hair, sparkling green eyes, and a heart as big as Texas. Her commanding presence kept all the men in the family on their toes. The only woman in a male household, she ran all of them like finely tuned instruments. She would give them hell when they disappointed her and give them love when they needed to lick their wounds. She had kept them going, being the strongest in mind and spirit.

"Yeah," he said, taking a sip of tea, "I know." He settled back in the swing, ready to hear her sympathize with him.

"You need to leave." His eyes shot open and he found his loving mother giving him a hardened stare. "You need to leave. You're driving us insane."

"What do you mean?"

"You're moping about the house, bringing us down. And, we're losing our friends. Just yesterday, you made that Ferguson woman cry when you were out with your father."

"She asked me what I thought of her new hairstyle. I told her the truth."

"Telling her it looked like something a cat coughed up wasn't truthful, it was downright mean." He shrugged, knowing his mother was right. If she wouldn't have been leaning up against him, disgusting him by reminding him he would never get to have Marlow lean against him that way, he would have told her it looked nice. "This from the man who, at the age of five, convinced his babysitter he was allowed to stay up until midnight. And the same man, who seduced a twenty-year-old when he was fifteen."

"How did you—"

"What do you think I am, stupid?" she asked and continued, not letting him answer the question. "And on top of everything else, you're irritating your father. No matter what your father's doing, there you are. You follow him around like a little puppy."

"Yeah, well, why didn't he say anything about it to me?"

"He's not tough enough," she said bluntly. "Besides, attacking a wounded male goes against some kind of code I still don't understand. Especially when a woman is involved."

"Heath," he said with disgust.

"Don't blame him. He confirmed my suspicions when I talked to him yesterday."

"How did you know?"

She laughed the same full-bodied laugh she always did, and he smiled a little. "Honey, no man alive drags his butt around like you have over anything else. From the way you've been acting and from what Heathcliff told me, that woman is worth her weight in gold."

"She doesn't weigh much," he said mulishly. "Why are you taking her side?"

"Why? This is the same woman who has finally reigned in the flirt of North Texas and is going to give me grandchildren."

"Ha! She wants nothing to do with me."

"You made her mad. You have to make up. I don't know any other woman who could have brought you to your knees. Now," she said, taking a newspaper clipping out of her shirt pocket, "some woman from Abilene sent this to you. Said it was real important you see this."

He opened up the folded clipping and noticed it was from the Sunday addition of the Abilene paper. The headline read Moore-Smith. What followed was an announcement by Ham, saying the two were getting married that June. Jealousy bubbled up and spiraled into rage. He left less than a week earlier. What the hell did she think she was doing marrying a man she had told him bored her to tears?

Well, we'll see about that. He got up without saying anything to his mother and prepared for a trip to Abilene the next morning.

No way in hell was his woman going to marry the appliance.

Chapter 17

Marlow studied the picture in her hands. She was wearing her cap and gown, her parents standing beside her. The day she had graduated from UT with her MBA she had been so sure she would take over Smith's Grocers. She looked at the boxes on her desk. Six years, two boxes. She'd be depressed if she thought about the years she wasted working here. She'd learned a lot over the past few years, but she should have had the nerve to leave years ago.

"Feeling melancholy?" Joey asked, leaning up against her doorjamb. Her belongings were already packed up.

"A little. I know I won't regret this, but," she sighed, "my first job was in one of our stores."

Joey walked into the office and then plopped down in one of the chairs in front of Marlow's desk.

"Yeah, I know. But we're going to make a splash in Dallas."

"I hope so." She placed the picture into the box. "Well, that's the last of it."

"We're both out of our apartments in December. I guess we need to start planning. We need to figure out in what part of the Metroplex we want to work. Then we can start researching apartments."

Joey wore an expectant smile and Marlow knew the one she returned fell short. Planning and plotting just didn't appeal to her at the moment.

"Don't worry, Marl, everything will work out." Joey walked around the desk, gave her a hug, and then left her alone with her box full of memories.

* * * *

Liam made it to Abilene in less than two and a half hours. He thanked God and his radar detector he'd made it alive and without any tickets. He stormed into the building, only to be brought up short by Ben Alden, the ex.

"Campbell, what the hell are you doing back here?"

"None of your damn business." *Okay, a little immature, but this was a man Marlow had married to make her father happy.* It chapped Liam's hide she considered him a bad risk.

"It is, if it has to do with Marlow," Ben said, crossing his arms across his chest.

"If it has to do with Marlow, then it's my business, not yours."

Both men studied each other in silence, and then Ben said, "I want to get one thing straight. You hurt her. She has forbidden me to hurt you. You do it again, I'm not asking."

"You can try."

Ben nodded and walked past him, brushing his shoulder against Liam's. The people gathered in the lobby to witness the altercation now shifted uncomfortably, wondering if they should leave or not. Liam ignored them and headed for Marlow's office. Little Ms. Marlow Jane and he were going to have it out, once and for all.

* * * *

Liam walked into the outer office to find Joey hoisting a box off her desk. The walls were now bare of her personal mementoes. She stopped when she saw him standing in the doorway, a sly smile curved her lips. She shifted the box from in front of her to her hip.

"Well, I see you got the announcement," she said.

"I figured you were the one who sent it. Did Marlow finally fire you?"

"No, I quit." He shot her a disbelieving look. "It's true. But there are a lot of changes happening around here. Marlow resigned too. I won't work for anyone else here. You got any job openings?"

Worry knotted his gut. *Was Marlow resigning to become Mrs. Moore?* He never thought she'd quit but he could tell Joey wasn't joking with him.

She gestured towards Marlow's door with her head. "She's in there, packing up her office. She might need help with some of those boxes."

Liam started towards the door. He turned to face her and said, "Thanks, I owe you."

"Yeah, well if you owe me, keep your brother out of my hair. That man is insane."

If he weren't so intent on confronting Marlow, he would have pursued that comment. But he had only one thing on his mind: getting Marlow.

He opened her door without knocking.

She didn't turn around when he opened the door; she just kept looking out her window at the Abilene landscape. It had been seven days since he had seen her and he couldn't get enough of the sight of her. She left her hair loose today and the ebony silk spilled past her shoulders and down to her waist. Instead of the boxy suits she usually wore, she had on a pair of jeans, which hugged her slender legs and ass. Contentment filled him, warmed him from the inside out.

"Oh, Joey," she said without turning around, "we need to look into hiring some movers. I don't relish the thought of moving ourselves."

"I'd be happy to help, I just need to know where you're moving, and when."

She turned around and gasped at the same time. Her blue eyes rounded in surprise.

"Liam."

"The one and only, babe." He shoved his hands into his jacket pockets to hide the fact they were shaking. He sauntered forward, trying to display a confidence he just didn't have. "Did you miss me?"

She swallowed twice and he could see the pulse in her neck fluttering.

"Well, you've only been gone a week."

He glanced around the room. "Seems I missed a lot while I've been gone."

"Yeah, well, I resigned." She busied herself with taping the box on top of her desk. "What are you doing back in Abilene?"

"What do you mean?"

She looked up. "I…I mean what are you doing back here? I thought you were finished." He shook his head. "Daddy turned down our ideas, Liam. There's nothing left."

"Yes, there is." He slowly, almost leisurely, walked around the desk.

"What?"

"You." She gave him a disbelieving look. "Really. I was

told if I wanted my parents to talk to me again, I needed to get out of the funk I was in."

"Funk?"

"Yeah, funk. You see, I took a few days off, went to Henrietta to visit the folks. They kicked me out of the house."

She shot him another disbelieving look and then busied herself with taping the box. He sighed, thinking he wasn't making any headway. Then, he noticed a tremor in her hands. Confidence bloomed within him.

"I was just hanging out at their house, you know. My mom told me to get out. No, really. You see it seems some of their female friends don't like me." She snorted, but still didn't say anything. "So, she kicked me out and told me to fix what was wrong."

"Really, and I suppose you think I can help you with that?" Was that hope he heard in her voice?

"Now that you mention it," he said as he moved in behind her, "I think you might be able to help." He inhaled her scent, lavender and Marlow, sweet mixed with spicy. Just one little whiff, and the blood in his head slid to his groin. He took shallow breaths to calm his racing heart. He had to keep his mind working.

"It seems my mother contacted Heath to find out what happened in the last few weeks. You know what he told her?" She shook her head but didn't turn around. Her hands had stilled on the box. "Heath told her I was mooning over some uptight, picture straightening little woman from Abilene."

Her intake of breath echoed in the silent office. His stomach jumped, his heart leaped in his chest.

"You want to know what I told her? I told her he was right. That I left part of me here in Abilene because I was too stupid to tell the woman I love her. I love her so much it scares the hell out of me. I love her so much, I thought I could walk away and give her what she wanted out of life. A husband, children. The problem was I realized *I* wanted to be that husband and I wanted to father her children. Marlow," he stopped because her silence caused a sliver of fear. Fear that she really didn't want him.

She turned around, slowly, unshed tears in her eyes, and hope soared. She swallowed, twice.

"You want to marry me?" she asked, her voice a hoarse whisper.

"Yeah, yeah I do, Ms. Smith. You're just going to cancel that engagement."

"No, Liam——"

"You're going to marry me and there's nothing more to discuss."

"Oh, really?" He had gained too much steam to hear the aggravated tone in her voice.

"Yeah, that's right. And, another thing, you better re-think this whole quitting your job thing. I'm not supporting you, woman."

"Liam, I love you." He smiled. "But, you tell me what to do again, and I'll kick your ass."

He looked at her for a second, and then started laughing. He grabbed her by the arms and dragged her forward. He bent his head, touching his lips to hers for just a quick peck.

"You're going to make an honest man out of me, aren't you?"

"I'll think about it," she said teasingly. Her hand slid up his chest, over his shoulder and onto the back of his head. She pulled his head down to hers, and just before their lips met, she said, "But I really insist you stick to consulting. No more moonlighting as a gigolo." He felt her smile as she kissed him, her tongue immediately tangling with his.

The kiss went straight to his cock, making his jeans uncomfortable. She went up on tiptoe, wrapping her leg behind his, tripping him. He fell, landing on the hard floor with a thud; Marlow knocked the air out of him when she landed on him.

"Now I have you where I want you," she said, as she straddled his hips, rocking against him. He groaned and she laughed. His balls tightened. As she looked down at him, her inky hair spilled around him, creating a curtain. He wound a few strands around his hand and gently pulled her face down to his.

"I don't want to be anyplace else, Ms. Smith." Then, he kissed her, but this time, he put everything he had felt the last few days into it as his lips touched hers. The frustration, the loneliness, his love fed through him to her in that one kiss. He pulled her just an inch away from him. "I love you, Marlow. I hope you forgive me for being such a butthead."

She chuckled, albeit watery. "I'll forgive you on one condition. I need help finding a job. Those hundred dollar tips are going to put a strain on my pocket book."

She leaned down and kissed him as he slid his hands to the bottom of her shirt, pulling it over her head and throwing it on the floor beside them. Marlow began clawing at the buttons on his shirt.

"I want to feel your skin, Liam, hurry," she said. She gave up trying to save the shirt and ripped it open, buttons flying in every direction. "Just put it on my bill."

A rumble of a laugh ended on a gasp as she kissed her way

to one of his nipples, circling it with her tongue.

"Marlow, baby, the door's not locked."

"Who cares?" She smiled up at him as she moved to his other nipple. "I've decided to start taking chances."

She slid down his body, kissing her way from his chest to his stomach. Finally, she was resting on her stomach between his legs, her face above the noticeable bulge in his jeans.

"Now, Mr. Jones, I think this type of constriction is probably not good for you." She yanked at the button fly all of them popped open. When she saw his cotton boxers, she tsked. "Really, Mr. Jones, what do you think you're doing? Wearing underwear. Isn't that against some gigolo code of honor?" The teasing in her voice coursed through him, draining any blood left in his brain.

She caressed him through the material. Heat seared through him. He could feel her breath on his cock, bringing his erection to an almost painful state. If Liam wouldn't have been so far gone, he would have heard the rattle of the doorknob, but a moment before the door swung open, Marlow had bent her head to place a kiss on him through the cotton.

"Marlow Jane Smith, what on earth are you doing?"

He turned his head to see her mother, her hand on the doorknob, her mouth open. "I would think you would know to at least lock the door." Clarice turned and slammed the door shut. He glanced down at Marlow, afraid she might be embarrassed, but all he saw was wry amusement. She pulled his briefs down and his pulsing erection sprang free. Leaning down, she licked the tip. He knew he was too close for this kind of thing. He wanted to come but not in her mouth. He wanted to be deep inside her, her muscles clenching him when he came. Before she could say anything, he pulled her down and rolled until he was on top of her. He wanted to love her slow and long.

"Marlow Jane," her mother called through the door. He thought he heard Joey snickering. "If you're not coming out, at least get up off the man and lock the door."

Epilogue

Marlow lay back, gathering her breath, as Liam collapsed beside her.

"You know, at some point, we have to eat," she said.

"We can order room service."

"Liam!"

"Really, babe, why go out to eat? We *live* in Dallas."

A week after leaving Abilene, Liam and Marlow eloped. They had spent the past week getting all the necessary paperwork in order, moved her stuff into his apartment, and Marlow settled in her new office. She and Joey joined the Campbell brothers as full partners.

After lunch, Liam whisked her out of the office, told everyone they were going to be out for the rest of the day. An hour later, a justice of the peace proclaimed them man and wife.

Then, he took her to the same hotel she had used the night they met and had rented the same exact suite. She watched him sit up and reach for the room service menu.

The same heat his body always inspired seared through her as she watched him walk across the room for a drink. His golden skin glowed in the candlelight, his hair was disheveled from their lovemaking; he could only be described as magnificent.

And, he was *hers*.

He turned and found her watching him. His lips curved into a knowing smile.

"Think you got what you paid for?"

"Oh, and then some." She looked her fill, starting at his broad chest, his flat abs, and then on to his lean hips. As she continued her assessment, her breath caught in her throat and then whooshed out of her when she saw his erection.

"What can I say, babe? You have that affect on me," he said with a chuckle.

Her face burned and she collapsed back on the bed.

"I don't think either one of our mothers is ever going to forgive us."

"Yes they will," he said toying with a few strands of her hair. "We just have to approach it the right way. We'll explain to them we didn't want to go through all the mess of a wedding." He took the ends of her hair and brushed them across her nipple. It puckered at first contact and he smiled. "That, even though they have no pictures or memories from the wedding, at least we're married. And, if they aren't nice to us, we'll never let them see their grandchildren."

A lump formed in her throat at the mention of children, causing her breath to catch. Liam must have noticed the tension in her body, because he stopped toying with her hair and looked up.

"You do want to have children, don't you, Marlow?" His voice soft and almost unsure.

"Yes, yes, I would love to have a couple of blonde boys," she said, as tears gathered in her eyes.

"Boys? I wanted some girls, with big blue eyes, just like their mamma." The tears spilled over and coursed down her cheeks. "Okay," Liam said, his voice taking on a panicked edge, "we can have boys."

She laughed and said, "Liam, I really don't think we have any say over that."

He leaned up on his elbow. The flickering light of the candles brought out the golden hue of his skin. Her heartbeat quickened as her eyes traveled down his chest. She brushed her hand against one of his copper nipples and smiled when he shuddered. Marlow could feel him studying her and she glanced up to see green fire dancing in his eyes.

"I really want to have some babies with you, Marlow. Now, Mrs. Campbell, I think all talk of families can wait. I'd rather get down to the business of making them." He covered her and she reveled in the feel of his hard body against hers. Marlow looked up at him, passion was burning hot in his eyes, mixed with tenderness.

"I love you, Liam."

"I love you, too. Now, about making those babies. I think we just might need a little more practice. In fact, we might just need to run quite a few drills."

ABOUT THE AUTHOR

Born to an Air Force family at an Army hospital, Melissa has always been a little screwy. She was further warped by her years of watching Monty Python movies and her strange family. From the time she read *To Kill a Mockingbird* in the seventh grade, she dreamed of being a writer. After years of struggling, trying to write short stories filled with angst, she finally listened to her college writing instructor, and allowed her natural comedic voice to shine through. She is a military wife and mother to two military brats and an adopted dog daughter, and lives wherever the military sticks them. Which, she is sure, will involve heat and bugs only seen on the Animal Discovery Channel. In her spare time, she reads, cooks, reads, travels, reads some more, and dreams of living somewhere the bugs die in the winter. She LOVES hearing from her readers through her website at
www.authormelissaschroeder.com.

For your reading pleasure, we welcome you to visit our web bookstore

WHISKEY CREEK PRESS

www.whiskeycreekpress.com